eggs

by jerry spinelli

LITTLE, BROWN AND COMPANY

New York ❧ Boston

Also by Jerry Spinelli:

The Bathwater Gang

Jason and Marceline

Maniac Magee

Space Station Seventh Grade

Who Put That Hair in My Toothbrush?

Little, Brown and Company

Hachette Book Group USA
1271 Avenue of the Americas, New York, NY 10020
Visit our Web site at www.lb-kids.com

First Edition: June 2007

Fiestaware 2000® is a registered trademark of the Homer Laughlin China Company.

Library of Congress Cataloging-in-Publication Data

Spinelli, Jerry.
Eggs / by Jerry Spinelli. — 1st ed.
p. cm.
Summary: Mourning the loss of his mother, nine-year-old David forms an unlikely friendship with independent, quirky thirteen-year-old Primrose, as the two help each other deal with what is missing in their lives.
ISBN-13: 978-0-316-16646-1
ISBN-10: 0-316-16646-4
[1. Friendship — Fiction. 2. Family life — Fiction.] I. Title.
PZ7.S75663Egg 2007
[Fic] — dc22
200602529

10 9 8 7 6 5 4 3 2 1

Q-FF

Printed in the United States of America

The text was set in Fairfield Light.

To my Gettysburg College classmates
1963

ACKNOWLEDGMENTS

It takes more than a writer to tell a story.
Many thanks to Catherine Balkin, Erin Gathrid,
Doug Fearn, Ben Spinelli, my editor Alvina Ling,
and my wife, Eileen.

eggs

"I don't even like eggs," David said.

"It's not just the eggs," said his grandmother.

"So what is it?" He no longer bothered to trim the surliness from his voice when speaking to her.

She thought for a moment. "Well, the activity. Participating." Her fists gripped the steering wheel. Her face was locked straight ahead. She was a rotten and terrified driver. "Making friends."

Make friends. Make friends. Same old garbage.

"I don't want to make friends."

"Everybody needs friends."

"Not me."

"We all do, David. We're all human."

"I'm not."

"No?"

"No."

3

"What might you be, then?"

"A moose."

He knew she wanted to give him a look, but she dared not take her eyes from the road. She settled for a sigh and a purse of the lips. "Now you're just being silly."

He let it hang there: "silly." He said nothing. Unreplied to, the word would get bigger and bigger, filling the car, suffocating her, forcing her to open her mouth and take it back, swallow it. That would be her punishment. Maybe then she would turn around, take him home, let the Easter Egg hunt go on without him. It wasn't even her idea anyway, it was his dad's. They could tell him the hunt was called off, or they got there too late.

She opened the window on her side. She said, "Would you like your window open?"

He did not answer.

"David?"

"No."

"Want the radio on?"

"No."

Question time. Try to get him to say yes.

"No."

"Are you ever going to smile again?"

4

"No."

"Are you a boy?"

"No."

Drat. Tricked. Didn't she know that tricks only made him hate her more? Wasn't the trick his mother had played on him enough? More than enough? Did the world have to go on playing tricks on him?

Houses, street corners went by. This was all his life had been since April 29 of last year: a ride to somewhere he did not want to go.

They were stopping, pulling to the curb at the end of a line of cars. "We'll have to walk from here. Looks like a good crowd," she said, her voice all peachy cheery, like nothing had ever happened. She came around to his side. She opened the door. He stared straight ahead.

"David? Ready?"

"No."

"They're going to start in ten minutes."

"Good for them."

She reached in. She touched his shoulder.

"Davey —"

He jerked away. "My name is David."

He did not look up into her face, but he knew she was closing her eyes, trying to be patient. "Excuse me. David. You know what your father said."

"Tell him we came and it was too crowded."

She made a thin, wincing smile. "I don't think so."

He looked at her. "We could dye some eggs ourselves and say that's what I found. *I'll* dye them. You won't have to do a thing."

She closed her eyes, smiled painfully, shook her head.

David kicked the door and got out. His father had told him to go, but he hadn't said anything about sticking to his grandmother. So he walked fast, zipping ahead of her. He knew she couldn't catch up.

He walked past the sliding board and merry-go-round and the tables and benches and grills in the picnic area. And he did something that he often did at times like this. He pretended. He pretended he was doing this for his mother. He pretended she was not lying in a grave in a faraway state, but that she had awakened him the next morning, while it was still dark, just as she had promised, and they had gone out to the lake to see the sun come up, just as she had promised.

2

Still groggy with sleep, Primrose fumbled for the curtain and pushed it aside. At first she thought she was seeing the morning sun — then she realized it was not the sun after all. It was an egg, dried and splattered upon the window. Then she remembered the thumps in the night, half-heard as she lay sleeping.

She wasn't surprised. They had egged the other place too. She knew that sooner or later her new place would be discovered. She didn't care. Let them throw a *farm*ful of eggs. They weren't going to stop her from having a room of her own.

She closed the curtain. She flung off the sheet and got up — and banged her head. "Oww!" she squawked, plopping back down. She kept forgetting the low ceiling. No matter. It was worth the crouching and duckwalking and occasional bump on her head.

She sat cross-legged on the bedroll. She looked around: curtains, beanbag chair, two-drawer dresser, her dad's picture, makeup tray, the neat stack of *House Beautifuls*, her sneakers side by side on the floor, just like anybody's. Sure, there was plenty more to do — like maybe a poster for the ceiling — but it was a good start. She grinned. She giggled. She pressed her fists into her chest. She whispered up the scale to a squeal: "A room of my *own!*"

She stared down at the bare knees protruding from her red-hemmed nightshirt. Last night was the third time she had slept here, but only the first in her nightshirt. You can't say a room is yours till you've slept in it in your nightshirt. That's what made last night so special. She giggled again.

For a good ten minutes she sat there, grinning, soaking it in. At last she folded the sheet, rolled up the bed, got dressed, and went outside.

The white of the egg-sun had slimed and dried down to the door handle. It looked like the silvery trail of a giant slug. Another egg splat yellowed the bumper.

She stepped back to the street. From the inside, with help from the curtains and a little imagination, it was easy to call it a room. But from the outside, from any angle, there was only one thing to call it: a rusty, tire-less 1977 Dodge van. A car. A junker.

But that would change. In her mind's eye Primrose saw a houselike paint job — maybe white with blue trim — and a little white picket fence and a patch of grass and a birdbath and flower boxes for the windows. She pictured it for a little longer and went into the house. The other house.

Even now, five years after moving here, the size of the house surprised her. It was so small that, upon first seeing it, she had assumed it was a garage. Some stubborn eye within her still looked about for the house, not believing this could be it. But it was. All four rooms of it: reading room, bedroom, kitchen, bathroom. She had once seen a picture of a movie star's clothes closet in *House Beautiful*. They gave the closet's dimensions. She found a ruler and measured her house. The closet was bigger.

The reading room, as always, was dark, soft, creepy, unreal. In the bedroom, her mother slept with Willy. They lay shoulder to shoulder, on their backs, sheet under chins. The sheet's rise and fall with her mother's breathing sometimes fooled Primrose into thinking Willy had come alive.

She looked down at them: one mother, one teddy bear. Take away the bear, and you'd swear that was one perfectly normal mother sleeping there. Well, not quite. The dark, hushed, spooky reading room — you'd have to take that away too. And the world's puniest house, which would make the cover of *House Ugly* if there were such a magazine. And the sign out front saying READER AND ADVISOR. And of course the bedroom, the *one and only* bedroom, the bedroom her mother actually, seriously, unbelievably (but believably too) expected to share with her teenage daughter. Take them all away and leave nothing but the lady in the bed, and then maybe you'd have yourself a normal everyday mother.

Hah! Until she woke up.

Primrose got a pitcher of soapy water, a spatula, and a rag from the kitchen and returned outside to tackle the egg splats. She hated removing egg splats. It was both difficult and degrading. Raw egg dried hard. Finished, she realized she was hungry.

3

David felt for the memento in his pocket, something he often did at rotten times. He did not want to be here. Did not want to be standing at the top of this hill with a million other yowling and shoving kids. Did not want to go racing down the hill. Did not want to hunt Easter eggs.

Did not.

The parents were behind, cheering on their little darlings. Lots of mothers. A whole flock of mothers. A man in a straw hat was talking through a bull-horn. The grass at the bottom of the hill was tall, shaggy. The man said that's where the eggs were, in the grass, in front of the trees. David stared and squinted as hard as he could, but darn if he could make out a single egg. He wondered if this whole thing was a trick just to get him to make friends.

"Get ready!" commanded the bullhorn voice. Several big kids darted forward. "Hey!" David heard himself say, but the big kids were already swaggering back to the line, laughing.

"All right. Once more. Get ready!"

Again the same kids broke. This time they went halfway down the hill. The bullhorn yelled at them, told them they would be kicked out if they did it again. They came back making honking noises. Big kids.

"One last time. Get . . . *rrrrready!*"

The man lowered the bullhorn and glared. There were giggles and flinches, but no one broke.

"Get . . . *set!*"

Glare. Silence. Eyes. Bullhorn. Wait. Wait. You could almost hear the eggs. David's toes tightened, and suddenly a kid was lurching down the hill, head over heels. He came trudging back up, yelling at the bullhorn, flinging his arm. "They pushed me! It doesn't count!" He grabbed another big kid and heaved him down the hill. "That's what they did!" Little kids shrieked with delight.

Somebody pushed another big kid. The kid went lurching, his legs wheeling as if on ice — *as if on a*

12

wet floor — and for a moment David felt his heart stop. That was how his mother died — from a slip.

Another kid popped out of the egg-hunt line, and another. The line was no longer a line, but a smear — surging and howling, "Eggs! Eggs!" The boldest of the little kids breaking away now, and the first kid yelling, "I can see 'em!" and the landslide was on, an avalanche of kids, the bullhorn bleating in vain: "Stop! Stop!"

Alone at the top, David screamed, "Hey! Didn'tcha ever hear of rules? Hey!"

David had always been a pretty law-abiding kid, but ever since April 29 of last year, he had become a stone stickler for rules (except his grandmother's).

And so, as the fastest kids were already plucking eggs from the grass, David remained at the top of the hill, calling, "Hey! . . . Hey!"

And now the bullhorn was aiming right at him and the voice was booming, "Young man! Go! Now!"

And down he went.

4

Eggs everywhere! Sky blue. Pink. Yellow. Lilac. Pastel treasures in a shaggy grass pie.

There were too many. He wanted them all. He wanted piles. He wanted armloads. He could not aim his attention at only one. He could not pick out the first.

Meanwhile, eggs were disappearing. Hands, as if triggered by his eyes, were snatching them as fast as he could spot them. There was a pink one! Gone. Over there! Gone. There! Gone. David was already breaking the Prime Rule of Easter Egg Hunting:

Be quick.

14

Gone. Gone. Gone. He was spinning himself silly. He moved nearer to the trees, looking for less busy areas. He knew now there would be no armloads. He would settle for some, several, a few. He saw big kids with three in each hand. They were ripping off the beautiful shells and chomping half an egg at a time and spewing white pieces as they laughed and pounced for more. Little kids were turning to the hilltop and hoisting their eggs and yelling, "Mommy! Look!"

And then, suddenly, he spotted one that everyone else was missing, buried in the grass, just a sliver of blue showing. He walked over to it casually, pretending he didn't see a thing. He knelt down, combing his fingers through the grass, pretending to search. He snatched it.

It was his! A sky-blue miracle in his hand. He whirled to the sun-washed hilltop, thrust the egg high — and then the sun was gone, blotted by the bulk of a big kid.

"Where'd you get it?" the kid said.

David pointed. "There."

The kid nodded. "That's what I figured. It's mine. I dropped it there." He held out his hand. "Fork it over."

Drat, thought David. What rotten luck. He forked it over. The kid walked away. His pockets were bulging.

By now kids were racing back up the hill, waving their treasures. David went on sweeping with his eyes, his sneakers. Nothing. Nothing but grass trampled flat.

He moved into the trees, beyond the last hunter. He knew the bullhorn man had said there were no eggs in the trees, but he didn't say you weren't allowed to look. And besides, it was the only hope left.

Leaves left over from last autumn crinkled underfoot. He peered into the shadows. It was different here, quiet, peaceful, indoors-like. The trees, so tall, so still, seemed to be waiting for something.

Somewhere car engines were starting up. He moved deeper into the shadows, wading through leaves, looking, looking . . . and *there* . . . straight ahead, a gleam of color —yellow — the clear, unmistakable roundness. Egg!

As he approached, he half-expected it to vanish or the sun-blotting kid to show up. Neither happened. What did happen was that he noticed how tall the egg was. It was standing. A solitary yellow egg, standing on one end of a large hump of brown leaves.

He knelt beside it. He picked it up. The first thing he noticed was the red marking that circled the egg on the end where it had stood. The second thing he noticed was the dark hole that was left when he lifted the egg. How could there be a hole in a pile of leaves? With his fingertip, he moved a leaf. Red appeared. He moved another leaf. Another. He froze.

Lips.

David knew he had a choice. He could stand up and walk away and forget it all, or he could move more leaves. One thing he had learned already: the marking on the egg had come from the red lipstick on the lips of the open, O-shaped mouth that had held the egg upright like a golf ball tee. He wondered what rules were involved here.

He began to brush away leaves. A chin came into view. A nose. Cheeks. Eyes. The eyes were closed. The eyelids were a glittery purple, the cheeks a blush of pink.

He brushed away leaves until the whole face was showing. A lady's face. Or a girl's. He wasn't sure.

Whichever, it was the most beautiful face he had ever seen.

He spoke to the beautiful face. "Are you sleeping?" The eyes did not open. He could not decide if he wanted them to open. The humped eyelids with their glittery purple were like tiny twin eggs, bird's eggs.

"Are you going to say something?"

The mouth did not move.

"You're dead, aren't you?"

The beautiful face was as still as the trees.

He was not afraid.

"My name is David. I'm nine. My mother died too. She hit her head. Her name was Carolyn Sue Limpert. We used to live in Minnesota. That's a state. I have a memento in my pocket, but nobody's allowed to see it." He thought for a moment. "I guess it's okay to show it to you." He took out the memento and held it before the closed, glittery eyes. They did not move. He returned the memento to his pocket.

A button on threads — daddy longlegs — came walking across the leaves onto a cheek. With a finger flick he sent it flying. His name was being called.

He stood. "I have to go now." He started to walk away. He stopped and came back to her. With great care he placed the yellow egg back on her mouth.

"Bye," he said, and ran.

When he saw that he was the last kid heading back up the hill, when he saw his grandmother's eyes wild with worry, he slowed down.

5

David had dreams that night. He kept hearing his mother's voice, calling him from the top of a sunlit hill. She was a shadow within thin tinted shells of eggs, speaking to him in sounds he did not understand. He saw leaves, a figure darkly rising, shedding dry leaves, rising silently as moss in wooded silence, and he tried and tried but he could not see her face.

There was no school the next day, Easter vacation. David bolted from the house as soon as he woke up. Let his grandmother figure out where he was. He rode his bike. He did not need directions. Even though the park was a mile away, he had biked there before. He had biked all over this new town of his. Perkiomen. Not that he really wanted to, but he wanted even less to be stuck in the house with his grandmother. Plus, biking was something you could do by yourself, which he usually was.

It was hard to pick out the hunting ground without all the people around, but when he walked his bike down the steep hill and onto the trampled grass, he knew he was there. Pastel chips of eggshell glittered in the thatch. He parked his bike at the tree line and reentered, it seemed for an instant, his dreams.

He went straight for the spot, and knew at once that something was wrong. The yellow egg was gone. And the leaves, still a pile, were shallow now, not heaped as before. Gingerly at first, then more forcefully, he kicked at the leaves, broomed them away with his foot until they lay flat and scattered on the ground. No lips. No eyes. No beautiful face. Nobody.

He went deeper into the trees, seeking tracks, scraps of clothing, evidence. Had animals carried her off in the night? Eaten her? Had someone found the body and notified the police? Yes, he decided, that was it. The police had come and taken photographs like in the movies and carried her away on a stretcher with a sheet over her from head to foot.

When he returned home his grandmother was in a tizzy. She talked in that whispery, patient voice of hers; she never yelled. As usual, she was full of whys. Why this? Why not that? She couldn't get it through her head that he didn't give a rat's rump about whys.

As usual, she slipped his father into it. "If you won't behave for my sake, David, or even your own, you should at least behave for your father's sake. He's trying his best to provide for you. That's why he drives all the way to Connecticut and back every week. That's why he's so tired all the time. He's overwhelmed."

His father's company needed him to manage a shopping mall in the state of Connecticut, over 200 miles away. He was home only on weekends. David knew exactly what "overwhelmed" meant. It meant less time for David.

She finally came to the end of her speech, saying, "I think you ought to stay in the house for the rest of the afternoon."

This was how she introduced all of her infrequent punishments: "I think you ought to . . ." More plea than command. She delivered punishment the way she drove a car: timid, nervous, afraid of a backfire. David's usual answer was, "I *don't* think I ought to . . ." And he would do as he pleased.

But this time he had a problem. He actually wanted to stay in the house, because he wanted to be there the instant the daily newspaper arrived. He was sure news of the body would be all over the front page. But staying in the house would give his grandmother the impression that he was obeying her, which was unthinkable. He could not leave. He could not stay.

He sat mired in the living room, wondering what to do. His grandmother went back to her housework. Every so often she would glance over at him. Her looks became more and more kindly, sympathetic. Any minute now she might decide to say, "Okay, David, you've stayed long enough. You can go out and play." And for the rest of her life she would smugly believe she had successfully punished then pardoned him. He could not allow it.

Think. Think.

He went into the kitchen and got a Mango Madness from the refrigerator. There were always bottles of Mango Madness on the bottom shelf. As he drank at the kitchen table, the answer came.

He popped up and swaggered past her as she was watering a plant. "Guess I'll go out," he said as if to himself and headed for the door. "David," she called, but she had lost and she knew it. One more limpid "David" and he was out the door, slamming it behind.

He took his time. She would not come to the door. She would not call after him. She would not do anything to upset him. She would sigh and close her eyes and remind herself that he had already had enough upset for a lifetime. It was all part of what she called "The Sadness." Nor would she tell his father, for he was already "overwhelmed."

David sauntered down the street. No one, not grandmothers, not anyone, could touch him. His mother's death had made him invincible.

6

The answer was so simple. All he had to do was wait outside for the paper girl, meet her down at the end of the block.

Hanging on the corner, he worked on his yo-yo stunts and thought about the paper. He was sure the entire front page would be filled with the story. There would be a big picture, maybe in color, showing the mound of leaves and the beautiful face and the yellow egg. And a headline with letters fat as fingers would say:

BODY FOUND IN PARK

He wondered if they would give her a name. He had never seen his mother's full name in print until he saw it in the newspaper:

CAROLYN SUE LIMPERT

At last he spotted the paper girl. He ran to her, got the paper, fell to his hands and knees, and spread it out right there on the sidewalk. There was a headline all right, but it said:

LITTLE LEAGUERS
READY TO ROLL

The picture was in black and white and showed a kid batting a baseball to his dad. No mention of a body in the park. Not on page one, or two, or any of the other pages.

At five o'clock David went up to his room and turned on the news. Nothing there. Later, in bed, he watched the eleven o'clock news. Not a peep.

Tuesday was more of the same: a ride to the park, newspaper, TV. He even widened his search at the park, in case it was animals after all, and they carried her off and maybe buried her so they could go back and dig her up whenever they got hungry, like squirrels with acorns. He found nothing that looked like a freshly dug hole.

Wednesday he called the police. He thought about biking to the station and talking to them in person, but he chickened out.

The voice on the other end said, "Police Department. Sergeant Wolf speaking."

David did not know what to say.

The voice repeated, "Sergeant Wolf speaking."

David said, "Uh —"

The voice said, "May I help you?"

David said, "Uh —"

Silence, except for a beep that sounded every few seconds.

"You've reached the Perkiomen Police Department. Do you wish to speak to the police?"

Beep . . . beep . . .

David blurted, "Did you find a body?"

More silence, more beeps.

The voice said, "Will you repeat that, please?"

27

"Did you find a body?"

"Who is calling, please?"

"David."

"David who?"

Why was this man asking questions? David was supposed to be asking the questions. "Did you find a body?"

"Did you *see* a body?"

"Maybe."

"Maybe? Where?"

"At the park, maybe."

"Where at the park?"

"The trees."

"And what did you say your last name was, David?"

David froze. He slammed down the phone. The receiver was wet from the sweat on his hands.

7

His grandmother was doing it again — mopping the kitchen floor. How many moppings did a floor need? Of all the things she did to torment him, this was the worst.

So he did what he always did at times like this. He walked right into the kitchen, across the wet floor to the sink. Then to the fridge. Then to the cereal cupboard. Not really looking for anything, just pretending. Pretending he didn't know she was there, pretending he didn't know she had stopped her mopping and was staring mournfully at him. He knew what she wanted to say — "David, please don't walk on the wet floor" — and he knew as well that she would never say it, never ever use those words to him. As he left the kitchen, he looked back just to enjoy the sight of his sneaker tracks all over the wet floor.

By the time he was halfway through the dining room, the enjoyment had worn off, and all that remained was a grim reminder. He ran to his room and slammed the door shut. He lay facedown on his bed. The tears came.

It was a wet floor that had killed his mother.

A wet floor where she worked.

A wet floor that a custodian had just finished mopping.

A wet floor that had no sign saying

WET FLOOR!!!

And along comes his mother.

It wasn't one of those spectacular head-over-heels cartwheel slips. It was just a little one. A tiny one. But it happened at the worst possible place: at the top of a stairway. Down she went. And even then, when she hit bottom, it wasn't the world's hardest bump on the head. Heck, David had had worse noggin-knockers himself. But again, it was in the worst possible spot, and that was that. She never woke up. Never called him "Davey" again. Never took him to see the sun rise.

It happened on April 29. Less than a year ago.

From that day forward, David had never even bruised a rule, much less broken one. (Except his grandmother's, of course, and her rules didn't count.) It was his most secret secret, one that he shared with no one on earth, not even the daylight. For David believed that if he went a long enough time without breaking a rule — a year, five years, twenty — piling up a million obediences, a billion — sooner or later, somehow, somewhere, a debt would be paid, a score would be settled, and his mother would come back.

8

Weeks went by. A month. Two. School was out.

David had stopped searching the newspaper. He went back to watching only cartoons and comedy shows and such on TV. He cut out his favorite comic strip, *Beetle Bailey*, and saved his favorites for his bedroom wall. He no longer went down the hill and into the trees.

Three days after school ended, he had to go with his grandmother to the Perkiomen Library. She was a volunteer reader for Summer Story Time. They walked. David stayed five paces behind.

Along the way they came upon a kid playing with a yo-yo. To David's horror, his grandmother stopped and said, "Well, hello there."

He knew what she was up to, trying to make friends for him. She just would not quit.

The kid stopped and looked up. "Hello." He couldn't yo-yo and talk at the same time. It was the ugliest yo-yo David had ever seen. Snot-green. What a geek.

"Do you live here?" his grandmother said, all sugar and smiles.

"Yeah."

"I see you're playing with a yo-yo."

"I just got it yesterday," said the kid.

David felt her bony fingers on his shoulder. "This is my grandson, David. What's your name?"

"Tim."

"Tim. Well, Tim, David moved here not too long ago. He doesn't know many people yet. But he sure loves to play with his yo-yo." She aimed her smile at him. "Don't you, David?"

"No," said David.

She chuckled. "He's just being modest. He's actually very good with a yo-yo. He can do lots of things."

The kid chirped up at her, "I can walk the dog!"

"Yippee," said David.

His grandmother ignored him. "Really?" she gushed. "Would you like to give us a demonstration?"

The kid didn't wait to be asked twice. He backed off a couple steps, took a deep breath and spun the

33

snot-green yo-yo down its string. It walked for about an inch, then lurched like a tire hitting a tree trunk and flopped onto its side.

David laughed.

His grandmother shot him a glare. "That was just for practice, wasn't it, Tim?"

"Yeah," said the kid. He tried it again. Same result. Then he did a surprising thing. He pulled the string loop off his finger, held the yo-yo out to David, and said, "Want to try?"

David sneered at the cheap toy and pushed it away. He unsnapped the yo-yo holster on his belt and drew his Spitfire. He knew he was playing into his grandmother's hands, but he couldn't help it. He ran a few test drops, then, with a hard snap of his wrist, sent her down for good. The spool of many colors — David had once counted nine — hummed as it spun an inch above the sidewalk, then a half inch, then a quarter. Then, ever so lightly, it kissed the concrete and, like a dog on a leash, walked smartly from one sidewalk crack to the next before scooting back up the string and into its master's hand.

With a disdainful sniff, David slipped off the

finger loop and holstered the yo-yo. The kid went gaga. "Wow!"

His grandmother cooed, "David! I never knew you were *that* good." Not surprising, since David had been careful not to show her his best stuff. "I'll bet Tim would love to take lessons from you."

David walked on, tossing his parting words over his shoulder. "I don't think so."

His grandmother stayed behind until they came to the library. At the door she whispered, "I can't believe you were so rude," and they went in.

The little kiddies and their mothers were already there, almost filling the Community Room. David took a seat in the back row. He folded his arms, put on a pout, and stared at the wall. He had no intention of listening to stupid stories, especially from his grandmother. He made one silent vow to himself: if she started reading *Mike Mulligan and His Steam Shovel*, he would walk up and rip it from her hands. Because that was the story his mother used to read to him at bedtime.

One last person came in, took a seat at the other end of the back row, and then the librarian introduced his grandmother. Lucky for her, she read

Brown Bear, Brown Bear. Halfway through, the little runts were yipping along with the story. Everybody but David clapped at the end.

Then she read *Green Eggs and Ham.* Then *Make Way for Ducklings.* Finally, the last one: *Goldilocks and the Three Bears.* About the time Goldilocks was peeping into the bears' house, David happened to look over at the other person in the last row. It was a girl. Teenager. She wore lime green shorts and a white shirt tied across her stomach and pink earrings down to her shoulders and brown hair unlike any David had ever seen before. It was pulled into a pair of woven ropes that hung halfway down her back. Bare feet. But the main thing was, her head was bowed and her eyes were shut as if she were sleeping.

About the time Goldilocks was sampling the porridge, David looked again. And kept looking.

As Goldilocks headed upstairs, David began moving quietly from seat to seat in the sleeper's direction.

Goldilocks was settling into Baby Bear's bed as David stopped two chairs away. The bears were staring at their porridge bowls as David lowered himself carefully to one knee and saw the roller skates on the chair beside her and tilted his head to get a better look at her face and her closed eyes, which he now saw were tinted with purple glitter like a pair of bird-size Easter eggs. And Baby Bear had just exclaimed, "Somebody has been sleeping in *my* bed!" when David let loose the scream of his life.

The shock wave from the scream sent Primrose toppling over backwards in her chair. From the floor she saw a sandy-haired little kid backing away, screeching, "You're *dead!* . . . You're *dead!* . . ."

Primrose felt her face, wiggled her fingers. She looked around at the stunned, wide-eyed faces. The kid seemed awful sure of himself. The look on his face. She was beginning to wonder.

"I am?" she said.

"I *saw* you. You *have* to be." He was no longer screeching, no longer backing up.

Primrose got to her feet, and twenty-five preschoolers screamed and clutched their mothers.

"Maybe I'm a ghost," she said.

More preschooler screams. Two fled the room.

"Ghosts don't exist," said the kid, who now seemed more angry than scared.

His voice sounded familiar. "Say that again," she told him and closed her eyes.

"Ghosts don't exist."

"Say 'My name is David.'"

"My name is David."

"I'm from Minnesota."

"I'm from Minnesota."

She smiled. She opened her eyes. He was staring at her, a blue, bold, unblinking stare. She remembered that in the park, even when he had truly believed her dead, he had not sounded afraid.

She pulled a card from her pocket. "Here," she said. She handed it to him, picked up her skates, and walked out.

The door was closing behind her, but she could not resist. She leaned back into the room and said, "Boo."

Preschoolers screamed.

The Waving Man

10

The next day David was biking around town, looking at street signs. By noon he had covered Perkiomen, up and down a hundred different streets. He was always careful to obey traffic lights and never go down one-way streets the wrong way. For the tenth time he stopped and pulled out the little white card she had given him. It was done in green ink in fancy handwriting. It said:

Madame Dufee
Reader and Advisor
"Meet Your Tomorrow Today"

Tulip Street

He pocketed the card and kept riding. He was thirsty.

About an hour later he found it. He coasted down the gentle slope of a street called Pratt to its dead end, and there it was, white letters on a black iron sign: Tulip Street. It felt like the corner of No-where and Noplace. Not only did Pratt end there, so did Tulip.

David coasted down Tulip. There were no houses, no sidewalks. Loose stones washed like roadside surf into weed fields. Sparrows flirted with the broken windows of an abandoned garage. A rustle in the weeds. Groundhog? Rat?

Ahead, on the left, was another garage. Or was it? A sign was jammed into the bare earth in front of it. Coasting closer, David saw that it was painted in the same fancy lettering as the card in his pocket:

*Reader
and
Advisor*

He stopped, lowered one foot to the glaring dust. The paint was peeling so bad on the place it looked like a camouflage jacket. A big old shoe-box–shaped junker van without wheels sat alongside. Splatters on the flat back end looked like dried egg.

David was torn. The foot on the pedal wanted to beat it out of there. The foot on the street wanted to stay, check it out. The place had a front door and one front window. Something hung over the window on the inside.

Just as David decided to beat it, the front door opened. A face peeked out — a lady's face topped by an explosion, a geyser of blonde hair. The lady made a cap bill of her hand to shade her eyes. "You have an appointment?"

What was she talking about? In the heat between them a dragonfly hovered like a miniature helicopter, then darted off. David grunted, "Huh?"

"No need to get mad," the lady called. "You're in luck. You don't need an appointment today." The door opened wider. "Come on. The flies are getting in."

David knew there were a million reasons why he should not go in, but none of them had made the turn onto Tulip Street. He parked his bike by the junker. "Does a girl live here?" he said.

The lady's feet were bare. Every toe had a ring. "Yes, yes. Now hurry. Flies."

45

David went in. A smell hit him — flowery, but old and sour. He found himself in the softest room he had ever seen. Floor, walls, ceiling — all were covered with carpets. It reminded him of a tent. There was no furniture. The door closed behind him, shutting out the daylight. He could not see.

"Sit." Her voice.

"Where?"

"Here." Hands on his shoulders pushed him gently forward, then down. "Here."

Nothing but rug beneath him. He sat.

"Who are you?" he said.

"Madame Dufee," she said. "Who else?"

A drape parted. Light. Her silhouette leaving. The drape closed. Dark again. Night in a box. David alone. Scared.

He held his hand before his eyes. Could not see it. Since April 29 of last year he had never been in total darkness, never allowed himself to be. In his bedroom, low by the baseboard, near the dresser, his Jiminy Cricket night-light glowed and smiled and tipped its top hat every night, all night long, while he slept.

He pulled his knees up. He shuddered. *Is a coffin like this? Are the walls moving in?* He reached out.

Humming. Beyond the dark she was humming. Or someone was. His mother used to hum. Carolyn Sue Limpert. He remembered once. He was on the stairs, playing dinosaurs and soldiers. Tyrannosaurus rex was eating soldiers — privates, sergeants — sometimes two at a time, chewing them up, and below him, in the dining room, his mother was setting the dinner table and humming. Folding napkins and placing plates and spoons and forks and humming while Tyrannosaurus rex ate the whole army, generals and all. Her humming had been the night-light of his life.

Flame flared. Madame Dufee was back with a candle. He could see now that a teddy bear had been sitting across from him the whole time, its button eyes forever astonished. She sat down and placed the candle on the floor between them. Her tornado-whipped hair was the same, but now the rest of her was lost in a robe of flowers, birds, and dragons with flaming tongues. Golden hoops you could pitch a baseball through hung from her earlobes. Before she tucked her feet under, toe rings glowed in the flickering light like ten tiny halos.

"Take off your shoe," she said.

Was she serious? "Which one?"

She frowned, thinking. "Which foot is your fa-vorite?"

He thought. "Right, I guess."

"Left," she said.

He removed his left sneaker.

"Sock too."

Sock too.

"Okay, lay down and gimme" — she flapped her fingers — "gimme."

He lay on his back and gave her his bare left foot. She tugged until the foot was close enough to the flame to feel its heat. Cupping his heel in one hand, she brought the foot up to her face. She ran a finger-tip across his sole. He shrieked, "Tickles!"

"Okay, okay," she said, "the worst is over."

For several minutes then she studied his foot, tilting it this way and that. She pressed the bottoms of his toes as if they were buttons. She poked his foot here, there. She began to nod. She closed her eyes. "Mm-hmm . . . mm-hmm . . ." She frowned with concentration. "I see . . . I see . . ."

"See what?" he said.

"I see . . . bread pudding."

"Huh?"

"Bread pudding."

"I don't like bread pudding."

"You will. You will sprinkle it with cinnamon and you will love it."

He doubted it. "Anything else?"

"I see . . . pretty babies . . . children . . . *grand-children* . . . a house with a white fence . . . a rocking chair on the porch . . ." Her concentration softened. She looked into his face. Fire-light danced in her eyes. She smiled. "*You*," she said, pointing, "you lucky buck. You are going to have a long and —"

Suddenly all went white — her face, the astonished bear, the room — as the front door flew open. A black silhouette stood in the blinding light, spoke:

"He's not a customer."

It was her.

"David from Minnesota," she said. "Come on."

He got up and went toward her, squinting against the glare.

"Shoe."

He went back, picked up his sneaker and sock.

To the ring-toed lady at the candle he said, "What did you see?"

Madame Dufee was about to speak, but the girl beat her to it. "A long and happy life. Now come on."

The girl clopped out the door. She wore skates. He followed. Both sat on the single shallow step, he to re-sneaker his foot, she to remove her skates.

"I saw the bike," she said. "I figured it was you." She stood in bare feet, no rings. "Want to see my room?"

"Okay."

She led him — *Was she serious?* — to the junker. She ran a finger over the petrified egg splats on the back. "I usually scrape them off first thing in the morning. Didn't get around to it today."

"Who did it?" said David.

"Hah!" She laughed. "Who didn't? They get their older brothers and sisters to drive them over."

"Why?"

She stared at him. "Why what?"

"Why do they do it?"

She looked up the street. "Who cares?" She looked at him. "I sure don't." She thrust a skate at the sky and yelled, "I don't care!" She reared back, hair ropes flying, and spit: "Ptoo!"

David laughed. He had never seen a girl spit before.

She opened the driver-side door. "Welcome to my room."

The first thing David noticed was that the steering wheel and seats were gone. He ducked in. She was right: it *was* a room, or as close to a room as the inside of a van could get. Curtains. Dresser. Rugs. Bed — well, a bedroll. Even a black-and-white polka-dot beanbag chair.

"Watch your head," she said. "What do you think?"

"Neat."

"I'm going to get some posters. Put them on the ceiling. I'm definitely going to paint the outside. Put a little white fence around it. Flower boxes. Like this." She opened a *House Beautiful* to a picture of a window with a flower box.

"Who's that?" David pointed to the picture on the dresser.

"That's my father. His name's Bob."

"Is he dead?"

"Why do you say that?"

David shrugged.

"Well, he's not. I just don't know exactly where he is, that's all."

David said, "I have a father."

"Give that kid a prize."

"He works in the state of Connecticut. That's two hundred miles away. He's the boss of a big mall. He only comes home on weekends. He's overwhelmed."

"That so?"

"Yeah." David sat on the beanbag chair. "I'm thirsty."

"Good for you."

"Don't you have anything to drink in this car?"

"It's a room, not a car."

"Well, do you?"

"You see a refrigerator?"

"No."

"So what do you want? A beer?"

"No. Mango Madness."

Her eyes shot open. "Really?"

"It's my favorite."

She wagged her head. "Amazing."

"What's amazing?"

"Me and a little kid runt like the same drink."

"I'm not little," he said. He leaned back into the beanbag chair. "Is that your mother in there?"

She glared at him. She snipped, "What makes you think she's my mother?"

"I don't know."

"Did I ever *say* she was my mother?"

"No."

"Did I ever call her Mom? Mommy?"

"No."

She glared another second, then laughed. "Yeah, she's my mother." She gave him a friendly smile. "She's goofy, huh?"

David giggled. "Yeah."

The smile vanished. "You calling my mother goofy?"

David froze. "No."

She laughed. "Why not? She *is* goofy."

David was going goofy with confusion. He took no more chances. He kept a blank expression on his face and said nothing.

"My mother is psychic," she said. "Scratch that. My mother *thinks* she's psychic."

He risked a question. "What's that?"

"It means she can, like, tell the future."

"She's a fortune-teller?"

"Yeah. She thinks."

"The sign says 'Reader.'" When he first saw it, he thought the person inside must be a reader for Summer Story Time, like his grandmother.

"That means she reads your palm. Tells you what your future will be."

"She read my foot. It tickled."

She snickered. "Yeah, sometimes she does that too. She says she's exploring new territory."

This was all new territory to David, this strange girl and her strange mother. "Are you psychic too?" he asked her.

She snorted. "Nah. Thank God. It's all bullcrap. I'd never want to be my mother." She was twisting her hair. "She lives in the clouds. In the future. I think all those palms got to her. Not me. I'm living now. Today." She laughed. "Plus!" She swatted at a fly with *House Beautiful*.

"Plus what?"

She pointed toward the garage-size house. "There's only one bedroom and one bed in there and I have to sleep with her and she *snores*."

She laughed. David took a chance to join in.

"So that's why I moved out," she said.

David had heard his grandmother snore once or twice, but never his mother. "Are you an only child?" he asked her.

"Yeah. You?"

"Yeah."

"Only way to fly."

"What's that mean?"

She sat cross-legged on the floor. "I don't know. A saying."

They were silent for a while, David floating in the polka dots of the giant black-and-white beanbag, feeling something good from long ago. At last he said to her, "Why aren't you dead?"

She looked at him; she laughed. "Don't look so heartbroken. If it'll make you feel better, I'll kill myself."

"You tricked me."

She rolled a skate into his foot. "Not really. I knew about the egg hunt. I went in the back way to get a couple of eggs for breakfast. I'm too old now to be in it. Not that I would ever go running down the hill with the rest of those idiots. And then" — she rolled the other skate — "I heard everybody coming and I saw the leaves . . ." She grinned.

"What?" he said.

"That bug. Boy, you don't know how hard it was to keep still with that thing crawling on my face."

"I flicked it off."

"I know."

David sat up. "You *did* trick me! You saw my memento!"

"Don't have a hernia. How could I see it? My eyes were shut. I was dead, remember?"

"You could've peeked."

"I didn't." She grinned again. Her grin seemed to say, *I know stuff you don't.* "So, are you going to show it to me now?"

"No."

"Do you have it on you?"

"Maybe. Maybe not." He *always* had it on him.

She grinned. "Is it from your mother?"

"No!" he shot back. "And nunna your business anyway."

She grinned some more. He was liking her less and less.

"So," she said, "want to know my name?"

David stared at the ceiling. He shrugged. "I don't care."

"Primrose."

He snickered. "Right."

"Really, that's it. Primrose. Ever hear such an ugly name?"

He did not answer. He would not get suckered into another trick.

She got her skates. "Come on." Outside, she put on the skates and stood, now taller than ever. She took a bill from her pocket, a twenty. She waved it before his nose, grinning. "Want a Mango Madness?"

"Where did you get that?"

"Can I see the memento?"

"No."

"You want to know where I got all this money, don't you?"

"No."

She cloppered across the dirt to the street. "I knew you did. But to find out, you have to come with me tonight. *Late* tonight." She looked back at him. "Are you allowed, little boy?"

"I can do anything I want," he said. *When my father isn't home*, he thought. "I'm not little."

"Good," she said. She pushed off. "Let's go get some Mango Madness."

He pushed off. Over the gravelly surface of Tulip Street, his bike tires were quieter than her skate wheels. Along the way, he sometimes thought to call her Primrose, but he did not for fear that it was a trick. He hoped it wasn't a trick. Because he thought it was the second-most-beautiful name he had ever heard.

12

Luckily, David's grandmother's house was an old-fashioned rancher, with all the rooms on one floor. To sneak off, all he had to do was lift up the screen and climb out. Which is what he did that night at precisely 9:30 P.M.

A voice came out of the dark. "Over here."

She was waiting in the alley. She turned on a flashlight, aimed at something — a wagon. A *big* wagon. The biggest wagon he had ever seen. Wood-slatted sides up past his waist. "Wow!" he said. "Where'd you get it?"

"Refrigerator John made it."

"Who's that?"

"You'll find out."

"Can I pull it?"

"Be my guest."

David pulled the wagon down the alley.

"It's really dark," he said.

"That's night for ya."

"Maybe you ought to shine the flashlight."

"Only when I need to."

"You sure it's not stealing?"

"I'm sure I'm not going to explain the whole thing again."

She had explained the whole thing that afternoon. They were going "shopping." That was her word. His word was trashpicking. Tomorrow was trash pickup day. Which meant, she had explained, everybody would have their trash out on the curbs tonight. So it was perfectly okay for them to come along and take whatever they wanted. And what they wanted was stuff she could sell at the Saturday flea market. So she could make enough money to buy paint for her room (the van). Counting what she had left over after buying their lunch (Mango Madnesses, chili dogs, sour cream and onion chips, beef sticks, Klondike bars), she figured she needed about forty-five dollars.

They came to the street, and a streetlight. David felt better.

She went straight for the curb at the end of a driveway. There were two trash cans and a tiny leaning rocking chair. The chair was leaning because it lacked one rocker. She picked it up. "Isn't this cute? For a two-year-old. I can sell it for five dollars if —" She set it down and took the lid from a trash can. She aimed the flashlight into it. "Ah-hah!" She pulled out the other rocker. She laid chair and rocker in the wagon. "Refrigerator John will fix it." She waved. "Onward, Nellie."

David was feeling less better. The streetlights, it turned out, were far apart, oases in a desert of darkness. He discovered his voice could substitute for light.

"What if somebody thinks we *are* robbers?" he said.

"I guess they'll shoot us," she said.

"Why is your hair that way?"

"What way's that?"

"Like ropes."

"They're called braids, for your information."

"Look like ropes to me."

"The better to strangle runts with."

She picked up a paperback book. *The Case of the China Doll.* Into the wagon.

"Does it hurt your mother to walk with those rings on her toes?" he said.

"Never asked her."

"How come you had the egg in your mouth that day?"

"I don't know. No reason. I just do goofy things sometimes."

A car roared by, radio booming, voice yelling, "Scavengers!"

"What's that?" he said.

"Us," she said.

A golf club went into the wagon.

"Why were you sleeping in the library with all those little kids?" he said.

"I was sleepy."

"Why, really?"

"I felt like it."

"Come on."

"You're too little to understand."

"I'm not little. Stop calling me little."

"Little."

He couldn't help it — he giggled.

She kicked a TV set. "Never take electrical stuff to sell. It never works and people bring it back and get mad at you."

"My mother wore a ring on her finger," he said, "but not her toes. And she wasn't goofy."

"That so?"

"Yeah. Her name was Carolyn Sue Limpert."

"I know. She got hit on the head."

"She slipped and fell on the wet spot because a guy was mopping and didn't put the sign up."

"Right."

"We were going to get up early the next morning and see the sun rise. On April thirtieth."

"Yeah?"

"Yeah. I don't let grown-ups touch me, except my dad. And I don't break rules."

She shone the flashlight in his face. "Why not?"

He pushed the light aside. "Can't tell."

She grinned. "You will. Someday."

She poked around with the flashlight beam till it found a lamp shade. Into the wagon. "Fifty cents, if I'm lucky."

"I don't like you," he said.

She chuckled. "Grumpy little runt. You probably don't like anybody."

"Yes, I do."

"Yeah? Who?"

"My dad."

"Congratulations. Who else?"

Silence.

She snickered. "So many, you don't know who to name first, huh?"

"I used to like lots of people in Minnesota."

"What about your grandmother?"

"She thinks she's my mother. Nobody's my mother."

The wagon wheels hummed softly over the street. "Same here," she said.

Primrose began kicking trash cans and shining the flashlight into front windows. "Stinky stuff tonight. What's the matter with you people? How am I supposed to make a living on this junk?"

Up ahead a light went on. Across the street a door opened. "Hey!" someone called. "Outta there! Git!"

"Git yourself," Primrose growled.

"They're gonna call the cops," said David.

"Let 'em," said Primrose.

David whined, "I'm tired of pulling."

"Oh great." Primrose yanked the handle from him. "Big help you are. It's what I get for bringing a baby along."

"I'm not a baby."

Two blocks later he became so sleepy he couldn't think of anything to do but climb into the wagon. He knew Primrose would pitch a fit but he didn't

64

care. He curled himself around the junk and closed his eyes.

Sure enough, the wagon came to a halt and Primrose screeched: "Out! Out!"

He pretended not to hear.

"Sen-sational," she snarled. "See if you ever come out with me again." He felt her hot, bitter breath in his ear. "Infant turd."

The rest of the night was a drowsy clatter. He was aware of her piling stuff all around and on top of him, but it might as well have been blankets for all he cared. Then there was a man's voice, and laughter, and the junk was leaving the wagon, and sometime later he too was leaving the wagon (lifted out of it and draped over his windowsill), and then there was the plump softness of his pillow beneath his head.

13

That was the first of many nights sneaking out, many nights with Primrose.

David got better at staying awake. Partly because Primrose made fun of him if he didn't, and partly because he slept later in the mornings. Primrose had a watch, and every night as she boosted him to the windowsill to return to his room, he would say, "What time is it?" It thrilled him to hear the answers: "Twelve-thirty." "One-seventeen." "One-forty-two."

One unforgettable night she said, "Three-twenty-two," and he yelped out loud before she clamped her hand over his mouth. That was the night they had gone to the all-night Dunkin' Donuts. Primrose, as usual, had coffee with her donuts. But this time, when David asked if he could have a cup too, she said okay. Even after adding three teaspoons of sugar and lots of cream, he still didn't like it much. But when he thought of the look on his grandmother's face if she knew he was out so late drinking coffee, it tasted better.

When he finally got to bed that night he could not sleep. The clock was inching toward four. A horrifying thought occurred to him. What if he stayed awake all night long, until the first glimmer of morning? Again and again he heard his mother's voice: *"We'll see the sun rise tomorrow."* He had promised himself he would never see the sun rise without her. Along with obeying rules, he believed that this promise would help bring her back.

And so, while sugar and caffeine partied in his veins, David pulled the pillow over his head and squeezed his eyes shut and prayed for sleep. When he awoke, the sun was coming through the top of his window.

Of course, his grandmother took notice. "David, you used to wake up before me," she said. "Why do you get up so late these days?"

He could see in her wincing smile that she thought it had something to do with The Sadness. He shrugged and let her believe it.

From then on, whenever he sneaked out, a paper-filled pillowcase took his place under the sheet. Primrose smirked when she heard about it. "Great decoy. Brilliant."

The way it usually worked, David would pretend to go to bed a little after nightfall, still wearing his clothes. Then he would wait for the signal from Primrose. The signal was "Baloney!" Primrose thought Baloney! was much funnier that the birdcall-type signal usually heard in the movies. Plus, she was sure no one had ever used Baloney! as a secret signal before, and she liked being the first person in history to do something.

One night the Baloney! sounded especially close. It really was. She was at the window, grinning. "Open the screen," she whispered.

David spent the first five minutes giggling as she pantomimed silent havoc: stomping on the floor, slamming drawers, opening the door, yelling down the hall. She spent another minute mocking his Jiminy Cricket night-light.

They watched his TV. The Late News. Late Sports. The Late Movie. Seeing the word "late" made David feel both giddy and proud. He was willing to bet that the geek up the street with the snot-green yo-yo never saw late anything on TV.

He put on his yo-yo belt and holster, poised himself like a gunfighter, told her to count to three, and showed her how fast he could whip out his many-colored Spitfire and skin the cat.

He showed her his all-time favorite *Beetle Bailey* strips, laminated by his father and hanging on the wall. She turned on the light and read every one. She kept laughing louder and louder, forcing David to clamp his hand over her mouth.

It was during a pillow fight that they heard footsteps coming down the hall. David jumped into bed; Primrose darted behind the door. The door opened. David's grandmother, in bathrobe and slippers, said, "David, my goodness. Still awake? Light on? TV? Is that the noise I hear?"

David said, "Yeah," and he tried to stop there; but behind the door, inches from his grandmother, Primrose had jammed her forefingers into the corners of her mouth and stretched her face into such a preposterous shape that David could absolutely not help himself: a laugh grenade exploded from his mouth and nose.

His grandmother looked baffled. David quickly croaked, "Something funny on TV." His grandmother beamed, and David knew why. It was the first time since moving here that he had laughed in her presence — and Primrose had tricked him into it.

"Well —," his grandmother said, oozing happy surprise, "shall I turn out the light?"

"No," he said.

"Okay." The way she looked at him, the way she tilted, David knew she wanted to dash across the room and hug him. He made his face say, *Don't try it.* She didn't. But she did say, "Night, Davey," and closed the door before he could say, "My name is David." At times like this it struck him how slick a grandmother could be.

They watched the Late Late Show. They sat on the bed, leaning back against the wall. Then Primrose sat in front of David, cross-legged, and David unwound the rubber band from the end of one of her braids, and then he unwound the braid itself and let the brown hair spill down her back. And then, after she showed him how, he tried it, parting a stream of hair into thirds and layering it left over, right over, left over, right over, the whole thing, finishing with the rubber band. She pulled it around front and examined it. "I've seen worse," she said.

He fell asleep then and did not know when she left. He did not see her turn off the TV and turn out the light. He did not hear her crying as she climbed out the window.

15

When they weren't "shopping" or dining at Dunkin' Donuts, they were roaming the aisles of the all-night Super Fresh supermarket or checking out the all-night 7-Eleven or hanging around Primrose's four-wheeled room or cruising the dark streets and alleys of town, she on her skates, he on his bike, sipping Mango Madness all the while. There was one place they were almost sure to go every night, sometimes for a few minutes, sometimes for hours: Refrigerator John's.

Refrigerator John did not measure up to his name. He was neither as tall nor as wide as a refrigerator. In fact, he was not a hair taller than Primrose, who backed up to him every night for measurement. "Any minute now," she would say, "I'm going to pass you."

"Have a cigar," he would say in a kidding effort to stunt her growth.

John knew something about stunted growth. His own right leg had been withered since birth. When he walked, the leg flapped out sideways, as though he were shaking a dog loose. "Hey, Shake-A-Leg!" teenage drivers would yell over thumping subwoofers and crackling mufflers as they hauled eggs down to Primrose's van.

"Yo, Johnny Junk!"

Sometimes Primrose was there, and she would scream back at them: "Hey, why don't you get out of the car and say that! Come on over here and say that!" They wouldn't, of course, so Primrose would turn to John, who would be grinning, and growl, "You don't *care* if they say that stuff? You're not even mad." And he would grin some more and say, "Why should I get mad? You're mad enough for everybody." And Primrose would get madder.

"You're not like your mother," John would say.

"Thank God," Primrose would say and roll her eyes.

"She's always in a good mood."

"That's her problem."

Refrigerator John would laugh. He had liked Primrose and her mother before he even met them, just from knowing they were moving into the old machine shop down the way and he would no longer be the only human inhabitant on April Street. He liked Primrose even more when he met her. She didn't seem to notice how short or gimpy he was. She looked him in the eye and talked to him. Sometimes she would plop herself down and watch TV and ignore him for hours until she said, "So what's for dinner?" She almost always wore a sourpuss, and for some reason he liked that too.

And now she was coming around with this kid David. The kid was only nine and about half Primrose's size, and it looked out of whack, the two of them together. But they seemed to get along. Maybe because he had a sourpuss to match hers.

John liked them both. Actually, he liked all kids. Of the two kinds of people — kids and grown-ups — he liked kids better. But kids didn't like him back. Little kids feared his floppy foot. Big kids mocked him.

From the outside, Refrigerator John's place looked like it was patched together from the junkyard that surrounded it. Cinder block here, plywood

74

there, tar paper there — he had done it with his own hands. He called it "the abode." The furnishings, from kitchen table to easy chairs, had come from appliance customers who had other stuff they wanted to get rid of.

No one had ever given John a TV, so for years he was quite content with a radio — until the two kids began coming around almost every night. Knowing he could not command them to stay off the streets, he decided to entice them to stay at his place as much as possible. He filled his freezer with frozen pizza, and stacked cartons of Mango Madness half-way to the ceiling. He hung a dartboard on the bathroom door and set a Monopoly game in the middle of the dining room table.

And he bought a TV. A 28-incher.

But it didn't work out quite the way he had expected.

16

They ate the pizza, drank the Mango Madness, and ignored the Monopoly. After a week of dart games, the bathroom door was full of holes. He took down the board. They fought over what TV shows to watch. When she got her way, David wouldn't watch. And vice versa.

At least once a night David said, "I don't like you." And she said, "Ditto."

On those rare occasions when they agreed to a program, they hardly ever saw it through to the end. Primrose could not let a show go by without a parade of comments.

Quiz shows: "Who let you in? That's the stupidest answer I ever heard."

Murder mysteries: "You deserve to get killed for wearing such stupid clothes, you idiot."

Situation comedies: "Oh, that was really funny. I can hardly control myself. Look how hard I'm laughing. I'm wetting myself. Ha-ha."

Talk shows: "You what? . . . You *what?*"

Half the time, with a final "This is too stupid," she would snatch the remote and punch off the POWER button.

"Hey!" David would shriek.

"It's *my* show," Primrose would retort. "I can turn it off if I want."

"Then put on something I want to see."

"It's my half hour. I can do anything I want with it."

If the boy reached for the remote, she would smack his wrist and he would bellow: "Refrigerator!"

But Refrigerator would be too busy laughing.

Sometimes the TV would lead to brief dialogues between the two. Much of what John knew about them came at times like these.

Once, as they watched a movie about two kids, Primrose said, "Best friends are stupid."

"I had a best friend in Minnesota," said the boy.

"Whoop-dee-doo."

"His name was Raymond. He came to my birthday party. We collected stuff together." He was braiding Primrose's hair. Sometimes he did it for hours on end. Braiding, undoing, rebraiding.

"Do you keep in touch with him?" said John.

"I'm allowed to call him long distance in Minnesota once a week if I want to."

"Do you?" said the girl, calling his bluff.

"I did the first couple weeks. But I didn't since a pretty long time ago."

"I knew it," she said. "And does he ever call you?"

"Not yet," said David.

She pulled the braid from his hand. "Hah. 'Course not. Why should he? He doesn't like you."

John said, "Maybe you'll find a new best friend around here."

David recaptured the braid and resumed weaving. He shrugged. "Maybe."

Whenever a grandmother appeared on screen, Primrose was sure to say, "Hey, Fridge, what do you think about a kid who hates his own grandmother?" John of course would not reply. He knew about the boy's mother dying, and the grandmother from whom he fled when the father wasn't home, which was a lot of nights. He wished the boy would flatly deny Primrose's claim, but all he ever did was offer a tepid revision: "I never said I hated her."

"Yeah, right," sneered Primrose. "And tell me you don't hate carrots."

One night the boy abruptly fired back: "And what do you think about a *girl* who hates her own *mother*?"

"Mother?" said Primrose blithely as she changed a channel. "What mother?"

A gusher of game show laughter spilled into the silence of the room.

The girl's father was another story. Long ago Primrose had proudly shown John his framed picture, said his name was Bob. Recently she had had a small copy made. She carried it in her pocket. While she said little of her mother except to complain, she was full of good words for her father. She constantly speculated on how he looked now, where he was living, what he was doing. Her mother, she said, had told her that her father had left when she was a baby. Primrose swore that she remembered his face, first smiling and then sad, hovering above her crib and saying, "Bye-bye, Primsy. I love you."

The boy would scoff. "You don't remember that. Babies can't remember."

Primrose would scoff back. "Not all babies are as dumb as you. I said I remember — I remember."

The boy wouldn't back down. "And anyway, even if you *did* remember seeing him, you couldn't remember *what* he said — " here his face would redden and jut into hers — "because babies *can't understand talk!*"

Primrose would grin smugly down her nose and calmly say, "I could," and turn away.

What was it with these two? The thirteen-year-old girl, the nine-year-old boy. What brought them together? Sometimes they acted their own ages, sometimes they switched. Sometimes both seemed to be nine, other times thirteen. Both were touchy, ready to squawk over nothing. They constantly crabbed at each other — yet at the same time he might be braiding her hair, or she might be making him lunch. Half the time they left John's place snarling, yet the next day there they were, together, knocking on his door.

And so he did not take their squabbling seriously. He laughed, as there was no depth to their attacks. They were throwing stones — yes — but they were

80

skipping them across the surface of each other's water. Flat and sharp-edged, the stones stung for only a moment, then sailed off. But as summer droned on he began to notice that some stones became heavier, became rocks, were dropped rather than skipped, were allowed to sink. One day in late July, a rock hit bottom.

17

John noticed that Primrose's photo-father was drawing increasing attention from the boy. They would be watching a crime movie, for example, and the boy would say, "Hey, maybe he's a private eye."

It went on like that:

"Maybe he's an astronaut."

"Maybe he's a cowboy."

"Maybe he's a salesman. Like my dad!"

Primrose's usual response was a smirk, though John could tell she liked some of his ideas. As for the boy, he was perfectly serious and obviously thought he was being helpful.

Then his speculations became more immediate. He would see a sports announcer on TV, or a game show host or a chef: "Hey, maybe *that's* him!" Primrose would groan and say, "He doesn't look anything like that." And the boy would hold his ground, and they would debate the whole thing, and sooner or later Primrose would whip out the pocket-size picture and slam it next to the face on the TV screen and growl, "There — stupid. Does it look like him now?"

As disgusted as she appeared to be, she was always ready to jump back into it the next time the boy said, "Hey, maybe —" For, however unintentionally, he was goading her to do one of her favorite things: talk about her father.

Then he got silly. During a show about a circus, he pointed to a preposterous-looking clown and said it. This time Primrose's anger was real. She ground her words into his face: "He's not a clown." The boy did not debate the point.

The following night they didn't show up till after eleven. Primrose went straight for the remote and turned on the TV. The kids were groaning because channel after channel was news, when suddenly John shouted, "Stop! Hold it there." He pulled up closer. "I'll be darned. It's the Waving Man."

"What?" said Primrose, but John's flapping hand quieted her as he focused intently on the screen. Channel Ten News was showing a shabby-looking man in a scraggly gray beard and baggy pants standing on the corner of a busy intersection, waving. Smiling and waving. When the news went on to something else, John told them, "That was the Waving Man. I saw him myself in the city a couple times."

"What's he waving at?" said David.

"The people driving by," said John. "He stands there every day during rush hour, waving at the cars. He waved at me once."

"He does it every day?"

"Far as I know."

"All year long? Even in the winter? When it's twenty degrees below zero?"

John nodded. "Always."

Primrose, who had been listening with increasing disbelief, said, "Why?"

John faced her. "Why does he wave?"

"Yeah, why?"

John looked at the ceiling, and shrugged. "I don't know."

"Is he nutso?"

"No, I don't think so."

"So why does he do it?"

John sighed in surrender. "Who knows? Maybe he's just friendly."

"That's stupid," she said. "I think he's just nutso. Like my mother."

"Your mother isn't nutso," said John. "She's just a little different."

Primrose snorted. "Hah! A *little*? Try living with her."

David said, "Hey — maybe the Waving Man will wave at you someday, Prim."

Primrose sneered. "Let him try it."

And then the boy said it: "Hey, maybe *he's* your dad!"

The girl was on him in a flash, pinning him to the sofa, mashing his face into the cushion. John rushed over and pulled her off. She flailed in his arms, still wanting to attack. The boy was crying. The girl was screaming, "My father is not a bum on the street! Don't ever mention my father again!"

The boy screamed back, wet-faced and red: "I hate you and your stupid crazy mother!"

"At least my mother's alive!"

For a moment the boy looked like he'd been poleaxed. But he recovered and picked up the TV remote and threw it. It would have hit her face if John had not blocked it with his forearm. This was different. This was ugly. He shook the girl by the

85

shoulders and thundered at them both: "Knock it off!"

Shocked, they fell quiet at once. *Now what?* he thought. He had zero experience in controlling and disciplining children. He had to say something, keep talking, divert them from each other. So he said the first thing that came to mind. He told them about the nightcrawlers.

Nightcrawlers

18

The girl was still twenty dollars short on her paint fund. Much of what she made at the flea market each Saturday she spent the following week on lunch for herself and the boy. She was a go-getting earner, but not a great saver. She had been pestering Refrigerator John for more ways to earn money, and that's why nightcrawlers came to mind as he banished the kids to opposite sides of the living room.

He let them fire a few more I-hate-you's at each other, ordered them to shut up, and told them he had been thinking about opening a bait shop. "Lotta people fish in the river around here, y'know. Get me some minnies and worms. Clear off a shelf in the corner of the workshop. Nail up a sign. All I need is somebody to catch the bait." He looked at one, then the other.

The boy sniffed. "You mean us?"

John nodded.

"How much?" said Primrose.

John thought. "Well, let's see. Regular worms are small and easy to catch. Maybe a nickel apiece. Minnies are small too, but harder to catch. Ten or fifteen cents. But what I'm really gonna need are nightcrawlers. Big *and* hard to catch." He thought some more. "Say, twenty cents each."

"What's a nightcrawler?" said the boy.

"A worm, *worm*," sneered Primrose.

"A big worm," said John. "I seen 'em a foot long."

The boy gasped. "Wow!" His face was returning to its normal color. He put his palms together and drew them apart till the space between seemed like a foot to him. "Wow!"

"They only come out at night," said John, "especially after a good rain. And there's a special way to catch them. If you do, somebody's got hisself a fat catfish."

"A quarter apiece," said the girl, always turning the screw.

John gazed thoughtfully at the ceiling. He nodded. "Okay."

"Does that go for me too?" said the boy. "If I catch a nightcrawler, do I get a quarter?"

"Sure do," said John. "Business is business."

The boy clapped. "All *right!*"

When the kids came by next day, John was ready with two flashlights. Each had a piece of red balloon stretched over the lens and secured by a rubber band. "Let's go outside," he said. "Time for school."

He led them into the sun-bright weed field that bordered much of Tulip Street. He stopped and stood for a minute, saying nothing. He grinned at the boy. "Feel anything?"

The boy was puzzled. "No."

John chuckled. "Just kiddin'." He pointed to the ground. "They're down there. Just a couple inches under your shoes." The boy looked down and gave a visible shudder. "Thing about nightcrawlers is," John said, "you can't feel them, but they can feel you. Leastways, when you're walking regular they can. Right now they can't, because we're still. So here's the first thing you gotta do —" He got down on his hands and knees, his bad leg splayed outward. "You gotta crawl along real slow and easy and quiet." His voice dropped to a whisper.

91

"No talking. Signal with your hands, or the lights."
The boy was on his own hands and knees beside
him. "Got it?"

The boy nodded. "Got it."

John squinted up at Primrose. "Okay. Now, second thing about nightcrawlers is, they're real sen-
sitive to light. They don't like it. Look here." He
twisted his forefinger into the dirt until he had
drilled a half-inch hole. "The crawler comes up
outta his hole except for one thing. His tail. The rest
of him's laying out on the ground, maybe all twelve
inches of him, but his tail's still in here." He looked
at David. "Know why?"

Primrose answered. "Quick getaway."

John jabbed his thumb up. "That's right. If he
sees your light — *httthhhpp*" — he made a worm-
down-the-hole sound — "he's gone."

He took the boy's flashlight; he held it before his
eyes. "But that's only if it's regular light. Y'see, the
thing about crawlers is" — he flickered the switch,
the rubber circle brightened — "*they can't see red
light.*" His eyes met theirs. The boy whispered,
"Wow!" Primrose said nothing, but was clearly impressed.

He went through the whole routine then: crawling, shining the red light, grabbing the worm at the burrow entrance. "Grab 'er between your fingers and hold 'er tight," he said. "You won't be able to pull 'er out right away, because the crawler digs into the sides of the hole and hangs on. They can be stubborn buggers."

The boy laughed. "Stubborn buggers!"

"Yep. But just be patient. Sooner or later she'll relax, and you can pull 'er out."

"How do you know it's a girl?" said the boy.

Primrose thumped him. "It's just a saying, dummy." She turned to John. "How do you know all this?"

John pushed heavily off his good leg and got himself upright. "Used to hunt 'em myself, before I got into appliances."

They walked back to the abode. Primrose said, "I'm not touching those things without gloves."

"Me neither," said the boy.

Two days later it rained.

19

They left John's abode at precisely ten o'clock that night, each with a flashlight, a pair of gardening gloves, and a plastic jug. The jugs were capped and hung from ropes that had been threaded through the jug handles and tied around their waists. Primrose also wore John's watch. John stood in the doorway as they headed down Tulip. "Eleven o'clock, y'hear? — or I'm coming."

"Don't wait up," Primrose sang.

"I'm not kidding, missy."

"I *heard* you."

The rain had stopped hours before, yet the night could not forget. A fine mist kissed their faces. The fields crackled around them and bloomed cool scents of weed and wet earth. There was neither moon nor streetlight, only a pair of tiny, fallen red planets bouncing along in utter blackness.

"Can't even see my house down there," said Primrose.

"I can't see anything," said David. He pinched the back of her shirt, held on.

"Okay — now," she said. John had told them to go about halfway and turn left. They entered the weeds.

As summer went on, David had stopped being afraid of the night. Of course, he never had been scared in Refrigerator John's or under the bright lights of the supermarket or 7-Eleven. But even on the streets — the occasional pools of light, the hum of the wagon wheels or his own bike or Primrose's skates, the warm yellow rectangles of neighborhood windows, the very firmness of the paving beneath his feet — he had come to feel at ease.

This was different. This was the first time they had left the street, the first time in such total darkness that David, looking ahead, could see no difference between earth and sky. The red smudges given by the capped flashlights might be good for hunting worms, but they gave little comfort to a nine-year-old

95

human. The mushy, musky ground; the wet weeds hugging his legs — it was like walking blindfolded through a swamp. Creepy. A moment came to him from long ago. He was walking down a dark hallway behind his mother, her hand trailing for him to hold. "Don't let go, Davey," she was saying. "Electricity went off, that's all." He held on tight.

He wished Primrose would say something. He crooked his finger through a belt loop on her jeans. "We're not breaking the law, are we?" he said.

"What law?"

"I don't know. I'm asking you."

She took her time replying. "Well, there is one law I can think of that we might be breaking. Maybe even two."

"What's that?"

"Hunting laws. See, there's two things. First, you need a license. Like to hunt deer and stuff, you know?"

"Yeah?"

"Yeah. And we don't have one."

"But these are worms."

"*Big* worms."

He wished she hadn't reminded him.

A particularly tall weed slid wetly across his arm.

At least, he hoped it was a weed. He crooked another finger into the belt loop. "Think we ought to turn back?"

"Wait a minute, I'm not done. The second thing is hunting season. Like, you can't go around hunting whatever you want all year 'round. Y'know?"

"No?"

"Heck no. You want to hunt for deer, there's a special season. Special season. Pheasants? Special season. Bears? Special season. Worms?" She shone the red light in his face.

"Special season?"

She poked him. "Brilliant."

"So is this worm-hunting season?"

"We missed it. It ended in June."

"Oh." David pulled Primrose to a stop by her belt loop. "Then I guess we *have* to go back, don't we?" Heavy on his mind was his vow never to break a rule.

Primrose scoffed and dragged him along. "Nah. We're okay as long as the worm warden doesn't catch us."

"*Worm* warden?"

"Yeah, he's like a policeman for hunters. He throws you in jail if he catches you hunting in the wrong season."

97

David stopped her again. "Primrose. *We can't.*"

She pulled him onward. "Don't be such a geek. The warden doesn't care about a couple of kids. He's out looking for big-time worm rustlers."

He let go of her. He screeched. "I'm *not* gonna break the law!"

There was silence. Then Primrose exploded with laughter that sent every worm along April Street *htthhhhpping* back into its hole. And David knew he had been tricked again. A kick to Primrose's leg did nothing to stem the laughter.

At last she settled down. "Oh sheesh" — she wiped her eyes — "you are so dumb. You must take a dumb pill every morning. You believe everything I say." When she shone her red light into David's scowling face, she broke out again. David turned to go back. She caught him by the collar. "Okay — okay —" She took a deep breath. "No more messing around. We gotta get serious." Another deep breath. "Come on."

He followed her into the blackness.

26

Primrose came to a halt. Turning the dim light on herself, she put a finger to her lips. She drew gloves from her pocket and pulled them on. So did David. She pointed to the ground and got down on her hands and knees. David, with a faint shudder, did likewise. They began crawling.

Wet blood-red stalks came at David like a nightmare, bumping his nose and slipping across his cheeks; damp leaves licked his ears. The sog soaked straight through to his knuckles and his knees. He hated worm hunting.

As instructed by Refrigerator John, they crawled in the same direction, side by side. Whatever worms showed up in their paths were theirs. The chirruping of a hundred unseen crickets masked their own rustle.

They had barely begun when Primrose pounced. She held up her hand. David's red beam revealed two inches of wiggle dangling from her gloved fingertips. An ordinary worm. She dumped it into her jug and in front of a proud grin held up five fingers: a nickel for her.

Then David saw one, another two-incher. He picked it up and dangled it in her face and stuck out his tongue. Into the jug. A nickel for him.

For the next several minutes they both collected a good handful of worms, all of them two- and three-inchers. David kept tabs on his growing wealth: twenty cents . . . twenty-five . . . thirty. He could now understand the profit in nightcrawlers: twenty-five cents in one swoop. Four, and you had a dollar.

But where were they? Refrigerator had said they would be all over the place. He was about to pick up another two-incher when his eye caught movement at the hazy edge of the light. He looked — and yelped "Snake!" as he leaped onto Primrose's back.

Primrose jumped to her feet to shed him, but he clung like a saddle, his arms around her neck, legs around her waist. She peeled him off, growling, "That was no snake, dummy. That was a nightcrawler. I saw it go back in its hole." She smacked his shoulder. "And that's probably where they all went, ya baby bigmouth." Her fist shook in front of his nose.

"If you punch me I'm calling nine-one-one."

"If I punch you, you won't be able to talk for a week. I never should've brought you along. I'm never gonna get my paint at this rate."

She abruptly stomped off in another direction. David hurried after her. "Hey, don't you lose me."

She whirled, she squeezed his shoulders, she shone her light in his eyes. "Are you gonna keep your mouth shut?"

"Yes."

"Are you gonna make me mad again?"

"No."

She shone the light on the watch. "Half an hour left. Crap." She dropped to her hands and knees and started crawling. David fell in beside her. Within seconds Primrose had stopped and signaled David to a halt. Five feet ahead of her, lying flat across the ground as easy as you please, was the longest worm David had ever seen. And that wasn't even all of it — one end was still in the hole. He stayed rock-still and held his breath while Primrose did as instructed: creeping ever closer, closer; holding the light steady, steady, till — *now!* — she clamped its tail at the hole and held on. The monster worm flailed about for a good minute before Primrose was able to pull it free.

With both hands she held it out full length. It looked as long as a school ruler and fat as a man's thumb. She poured it into her jug and flashed five fingers five times. Twenty-five cents.

David started crawling and was promptly rewarded with a long, fat one in his own path. In his haste, he moved too fast, jerked the flashlight, and — *httthhhpp* — the worm was gone. Primrose made a mocking snort. David stuck out his tongue and pushed on. He'd show her.

The next nightcrawler he came to, he did it right: slow, silent, clamp the tail. Yes! He had it. It looked longer than hers, maybe a world record. He reached over and waggled it in her face, dumped it into his jug, and paused to calculate. Counting the two-inchers, he was up to fifty-five cents now.

He plowed on, ignoring weeds and wet, spurning the two-inch runts, flicking them aside. He was going for big game now. *There* was one. Got it! *There*. Got it!

Compared to Easter eggs, worms were a snap. They were still following parallel paths, but they were no longer side by side. When one stopped to nab a worm, the other moved ahead. It was a race.

Quarter by quarter, David's total rose. Unlike Primrose, he had nothing particular in mind to spend his money on. He just loved the idea of accumulating it. If there were so many nightcrawlers in this small area, think how many there were all up and down Tulip Street. He could make a million!

He was up to three dollars and sixty cents when he spotted the next victim, a fat ten-incher up ahead and a little to the left. Closing in slowly on his prey, he pounced on one end — just as another gloved hand — Primrose's — snatched the other end. They lifted together, the worm like a short slick jump rope between them.

"Let go!" hissed Primrose.

"*You* let go," hissed David.

"*I* saw it first," growled Primrose.

"*I* did," growled David.

Primrose pulled. David pulled. The ten-inch worm became an eleven-incher.

"I need the money," snarled Primrose.

"So do I," snarled David.

"I'll spit on *you*!" screeched David.

"I'll spit on you if you don't let go!" screeched Primrose.

They stood. Primrose pulled. David pulled.

Twelve inches.

"It's *mine*!" roared Primrose.

"It's *mine*!" roared David.

She pulled. He pulled.

Thp.

Each now held six inches of flailing nightcrawler.

"See what you did!" yelled Primrose. She smacked David with her half.

David threw his half at her. "*You* did it! You're greedy! It was my worm and you took it!" With the hand speed of a yo-yo ace, David flipped the lid off Primrose's jug, turned it over and shook it.

By the time Primrose reclaimed the jug, a half-dozen ten-inchers were on the ground crawling back into the night.

In the beam from David's flashlight her eyes burned like a demon's. She stepped toward him. He backed up. She was about to take another step, but halted. She smiled evilly. She held her flashlight before him. "Take a good look," she said. As David

104

stared, he was impressed by the perfect red round-ness of the disc. He wondered why worms couldn't see it. Primrose's voice, seeming to come from the red disc, said liltingly, "Have a nice night." And the light went out.

David raised his own light, pointed it. She was moving off, reduced already to a shoulder and a jug rope at the dissolving limit of the red beam. He tore off the rubber cap and jabbed the fresh light out-ward. She was gone. He heard a rustle. There? . . . There? . . . His light showed only weeds and night.

21

The clock on the wall said 10:55 when Refrigerator John heard the screams. A moment later he was lurching down Tulip, cursing his bad leg. He veered into the weeds, the beam of his flashlight probing the night, homing in on the shrill cries.

He found the boy screaming with his eyes shut and his flashlight thrust upward, its pitiful beam vanishing mere inches above his head into the black vastness. "David!" John barked and took hold of him; impossibly, the screaming got louder. The boy fought, flailed his flashlight. Only when John pinned his arms and gathered him in and smothered him to his own body did the boy release his terror and sob, "Mommy . . . Mommy . . ." into his chest. The boy clung to him with surprising strength.

John held him there until the sobbing and trembling ceased. Fearfully then, having no idea what had happened, he called out Primrose's name. He prayed he would not have to call a second time. A sniffle in the dark, a rustling to the right, and his answered prayer walked into the light. Her glistening, gaping eyes; the hunched stiffness of her shoulders; and the cold terror on her face told him no reproach was needed. A lesson had been learned.

On the way back to the abode, the boy told what had happened. John marveled that such combat could result from a broken worm. He told them now what he should have told them before. "When a nightcrawler splits," he said, "the head end grows a new tail and the tail end grows a new head, and there you go — two new worms."

They both went, "Wow!"

Fifteen minutes later they were sipping hot chocolate. The boy had suggested it. Primrose's response — "In *July?*" — was more reflex than protest, and as it turned out, the boy was right. Hot chocolate was perfect for the moment.

Thirty minutes later the kids were squabbling over the TV. Refrigerator John sat back and relaxed and found reassurance in their return to the usual bickering. He suspected it was no accident, that some instinct beyond their years was driving them onto safe, familiar ground.

An hour later the boy was braiding her hair and she was grousing because he was pulling too hard.

Painted Windows

22

The first Saturday in August featured perfect flea-market clouds: sun-blockers but not rain-makers. The tables on the gravel acre along Ridge Pike displayed everything from watches to monkey wrenches.

One of the tables was rented by Refrigerator John, who in turn donated a third of his space to Primrose. David helped arrange the wares from their Thursday night shopping sprees. One of them was a toilet seat. A sign taped to it said, WOULDN'T THIS MAKE A CHARMING PICTURE FRAME?

There were also two paperback mystery novels, a painting of a bullfighter on velvet, an old blue-green Coke bottle, five baseball cards, a hubcap, an orange-colored bowl, a vase, a beaded lizard-looking pocketbook, and, under the table, the child's rocking chair that John had repaired.

Primrose was even grumpier than usual this day. John had decided not to have a bait business after all, so there was no market for paint money, and the customers strolling by the tables were mostly the same ones she saw every week. "Lookers, not buyers," John called them.

Lookers drifted sideways toward the table, never facing it squarely, never quite standing still, moving along even as they eyed the goods. Sometimes they gave a quick glance and were gone, sometimes a slower broom-sweep of the eyes. Occasionally a pair of eyes would land on a particular object, stare a moment, then look up at Primrose, as if to see what sort of oddball would actually ask money for such a thing. Even more rarely, someone would pick up an object and say, "How much?" Primrose's heart would quicken as she told them the price, and sink as they set it back down and walked off.

Early in the summer Primrose had taken John's advice and treated each table approach like a golden opportunity. She would rise from her chair, stand smartly behind the table and smile as the person looked over the merchandise and walked off. As the summer went on she dropped first the smile, then the smart pose. Now it took the sight of an open wallet to get her out of the chair. She slumped and grumped and stared into outer space and muttered with the regularity of a grandfather clock, "This business sucks."

Half the morning had gone by on this day when a shopper finally held up something — the Coke bottle — and said, "How much?"

"What do you care?" Primrose snarled.

The shopper gaped disbelievingly at the slouching girl, set the bottle down, and left.

To the next one who said, "How much?" Primrose answered, "A thousand dollars."

By eleven o'clock she was challenging nearly everyone who came near the table.

"You gonna look or you gonna buy?"

"You touch it, you buy it."

"Whatta *you* lookin' at?"

When he wasn't laughing, John was begging her to stop: "You're ruining my business." Meanwhile, word about the rude teenager spread across the fleet of tables.

Primrose's behavior was neither new nor entertaining to David, so he occupied himself by eating. Every half hour he visited the vending truck. By eleven o'clock his stomach was stuffed, his pocket empty of all but a dime.

What could he buy for a dime?

He wandered among the tables, scanning the goods: clothes, knickknacks, books, tools, toys, utensils. When he came to a table half-covered with framed black-and-white photographs, he barely gave it a glance — then stopped cold. He came closer. The pictures were all of people's faces. The frames were fancy, tinted with gold or silver. They came in many sizes.

At least half of them — ten, he counted — were pictures of the same man, like TV sets in a store all turned to the same channel. And here was the shocker: each one looked exactly like the little one in Primrose's pocket and the bigger one on her dresser in her four-wheeled room. The same handsome face. The same mustache. The same sly, slightly tilted smile. The same black, shiny, combed-back hair.

Primrose's father.

What was a picture of Primrose's father doing here? Why were they selling it? Why would anyone other than Primrose or her mother want to buy it?

"See something you like?" said the lady behind the table.

114

David didn't know what to say.

"Looking for a present for somebody?" The lady was eating a hot dog. A spot of mustard gave her upper lip a yellow mole. "Your mother maybe?"

"No."

She let him look awhile. She bit into the hot dog. "This ain't used junk like most of the tables. This stuff's new."

David said nothing.

She pointed with the hot dog. "That there's a nice one you're looking at. Only three bucks."

Three bucks for Primrose's father's picture.

"Okay, for you, two-fifty."

David said, "How come you're selling his picture?"

"I'm not," said the lady. Her tongue, like a nightcrawler, slid out, poked around her upper lip till the yellow spot was gone — *httthhhp* — back into its hole. "It's the frames I'm selling, not the pictures."

"I just want a picture," said David.

"Two bucks, you get the whole shebang."

David held up his dime. "This is all I have."

A voice croaked, "Give the kid a picture." The voice came from an old man in a lawn chair. He was eating something out of a plastic cup.

The lady growled, "What am I, Santa Claus?"

115

"Give it to him."

The lady glared at the old man, glared at David. She snorted like a horse and snatched one of the small silvery frames. She worked out the picture and jabbed it, scowling, at David. "Merry Christmas."

David took it and walked away. And now he wondered: Why? Why had he asked for it? What was he going to do with it? He didn't know. He stared at the picture. Could he be wrong? No. Thanks to Primrose, he had seen the face too many times to be wrong. This was the man, all right. Her father. Bob.

So why wasn't he racing to her and shouting, "Primrose, look, your father's picture! It's all over that table there!"? Because something didn't feel right. Something so wispy it would not fill the hollow of a thought. Something that made him want to drape a sheet over the table of gold and silver frames.

Across a dozen tables he could see Primrose. She was lobbing popcorn at the backs of people who failed to stop at her table. He put the picture in his pocket.

Minutes later it was Primrose who came running. She was waving money. "Look! Twenty-five *bucks!*" Some lady bought the orange bowl. She said it's called Fiestaware and she has a whole set of it except for the bowl, and she said would I take twenty-five dollars for it." She grabbed his arm. "Come on. We're packing up. We're going for paint!"

23

David just could not make himself do it. He put down his brush. "Primrose, are you *sure?*"

She looked down from the roof. "If you ask me that one more time."

"But it feels so weird."

"You're going to *look* weird with a white face in about two seconds."

"But who ever heard of a bedroom without windows? You have to have at least one."

"Why? So the egg throwers can look in at me?"

"So you can look out."

"There's nothing to look out *at*. Paint."

It had been hard enough to paint the side windows. But the last remaining window? The most important window of all?

Primrose thumped across the roof on her knees and with an angry swat left a three-foot track of Buten's white primer across the front windshield. "There go your excuses," she growled. "Now finish it."

Reluctantly, David took up his brush and, standing on a chair, began painting the windshield. The last thing he saw inside before the last brushstroke was the propped-up picture on Primrose's dresser. He had wanted to ask his father about it, but he would not be home for days, and David did not have the patience to wait. So he had resorted to his grandmother.

First he asked her if she knew that picture frames were sold with people's pictures already in them. His grandmother, who was snipping the stems of flowers from the backyard, simply stared at him for a moment, shocked — and overjoyed — that he would ask her a question. She quickly recovered and said yes, she knew that. David walked away. If he had to speak to her, at least he would do it in pieces, and if possible at her inconvenience.

Later he caught her as she was talking on the phone. "Why do they do it?" he said.

"Just a second," she said into the phone, not at all

irritably, and cupped her hand over the receiver. "Do what, David?"

"Put pictures in the frames."

"So they can give the customer an idea how their own picture would look in the frame."

She was heading out the door for her evening walk when he asked what kind of people they used for those pictures. "Oh, usually models or movie stars," she said. She waited at the door, her expression saying, *I like you talking to me. Please ask me more.*

As she watched her favorite TV show that night, he thrust the picture at her. "Know who this is?"

She hesitated, then dared to take it from his hand. She lowered the volume with the remote control. She nodded, smiling. "This is Clark Gable. He was a movie star many years ago."

He took the picture back. It bugged him that he could not annoy her. "How old is he?"

"Oh, he died some time ago. If he were living, I guess he'd be in his nineties, maybe older."

"His name's not Bob?"

"Bob?" She stared at the picture. "No, I'm sure it's Clark Gable. He was known as the 'King of the Movies.'"

And not Primrose's father, David had fully realized in bed that night. *Primrose thinks he's her father — but he's not. She's wrong.*

It took them most of the day to lay a primer and final coat. Nothing on the outside showed that wasn't white: wheel stumps, windows, fenders, everything.

"Looks dumb," said David.

"It won't," said Primrose. "It's nowhere near . . . uh-oh." She was looking toward the street. A long, chromey car was pulling up to the house. A lady in black skintight pants got out, followed by a small, yipping, long-haired brown-and-yellow dog. The lady pointed to the front yard, which was indistinguishable from the dirt and gravel driveway. "Poop here, Mimi," she said. Mimi pooped, and the two of them went to the front door. The dog looked at Primrose and David, the lady did not. The dog yipped. They entered the house.

Primrose picked up a paint stirrer, walked over to Mimi's warm sculpture, lifted it carefully from the dirt, and deposited it on the backseat floor of the long car. "C'mon," she said. "Wait'll you see this."

She led him (by the hand, to David's surprise) around the house — "Shhh . . . tiptoe" — and in the back door. At the drapery wall to the reading room, she knelt and pulled him down. She drew the drape aside an inch or two.

Madame Dufee, Mimi the dog, and the black-legged lady were sitting on the rug. Madame Dufee had one of Mimi's paws in her hand. She appeared to be intently studying the paw. She began to nod.

"Yes . . . yes . . . I see wonderful things. A long and happy life." The dog yipped.

Primrose got up, no longer trying to be quiet, said aloud, "You believe it?" and went out the back door.

They sat in the van, the doors left open as they had been all during the painting. "I don't know who's worse," said Primrose, "my mother or that weasel lady."

"She came before?" said David.

"Yeah. She comes a couple times a year. First time she came she had a different dog. Guess it didn't have such a long and happy life after all." Primrose lay back and stared at the ceiling. She balled her fists and pounded the floor. "Damn!" She jumped up. She swatted her *House Beautifuls* and sent them flying like paper ducks. "Why can't I just have a nice, normal mother like everybody else?" She stared at David, yet seemed unaware of the irony of her question. "A mother that cooks dinner. That takes me places. That buys me stuff. Hah!" Her laugh was cold.

"Those rings on her feet you saw? Know where she got them? From *me*. I found them. I was going to sell them at the flea market. It's everything. Clothes. Combs. Hah — the stupid *teddy bear*?" She rammed her thumb into her chest. "Mine!" She flung herself outside, ranting. "*She* takes *my* stuff. My mother. Who's the *daughter* around here anyway? *I'm* supposed to take *her* stuff!"

She stomped twice around the van, then came back in. "You know what's funny? You know what's *really* funny?"

David, wide-eyed, shook his head. "I'll tell you what's really funny. She" — she pointed out the door — "she tells everybody the same thing. 'I see a long and happy life.' Doesn't matter who. You could be ready to croak any minute. 'A long and happy life.' A lobster heading for the pot. 'A long and happy life.'"

She kept saying it in a funny way, her head wobbling like a puppet's, and David could not keep a laugh gob from popping out. Primrose didn't seem to notice. "Well, while she's telling everybody else what a long and happy life they're gonna have, what kind of a life am *I* having? Huh? What about *my* future? Huh? I'll tell you what."

She held out her hand. She pretended to trace lines on the palm. "Ah, yes, here we are. I see . . . I see . . . a short and crappy life." She gurgled up some spit, reared back, and sent a hocker flying out the door. "Ptoo! *That's* what I get!"

She left the car again. She was pacing, flinging her arms, kicking stones. "She's nutso. A crackpot. Like that nutcake waving at cars all day." She bent over and flapped her arm goofily at the horizon. As she stomped around the van, David tracked her passing one door, then the other. "I want —" She came back in. "You saw me at the library, remember?"

David nodded.

"You know why I was there? Huh?"

David shook his head.

"I was there because I never went to sleep with my mother reading to me." She flopped onto the beanbag chair. "Did you?"

David nodded.

"Right. So did everybody else — except me. I try

124

it a couple times every summer. I go to Summer Story Time. I close my eyes. I try to pretend the voice is my mother's. But it never works. I just keep hearing the story and hearing the story and I never get to sleep." She snapped her face away from him. She slumped in the beanbag chair.

In his mind David heard the old familiar words: "Mike Mulligan had a steam shovel, a beautiful red steam shovel. Her name was Mary Anne. . . ." How those words used to spin the drowsies about him night after night when he was little. Even now it tickled him that a steam shovel had a girl's name. He felt guilty for having such a warm memory in the presence of Primrose's pain. He wished he could make her feel better, but he could not think of anything to say.

She was subdued now, dreamy. She reached for the framed portrait. She stared for a long time at the picture in her lap, and David understood that a great and terrible secret had fallen to him. He had been given custody of Primrose's dream, her heart. He understood that he could not tell her that he knew the truth. Not ever.

24

For two full weeks Margaret Limpert wrestled with the question: Should she or should she not ask David to go with her to Midsummer Night's Scream?

Though she knew that grandmothers were welcome, it annoyed her that the annual scary story night at the library was billed as a parent and child event. For that matter, life itself was billed as a parent-child event: grandparents were not exactly banned, but neither were they invited. They were allowed. Grandparents were substitutes, stand-ins, expected to step in and play a role to perfection when the star was ill.

But what happened when the star was more than ill?

When her son's wife had died, Margaret Limpert had grieved as long and deeply as anyone. She had loved Carolyn as her own flesh and blood, and when David and his father came to live in her house, David became her new son in her mind and heart.

It didn't take him long to set her straight.

From the minute he arrived, he had been grumpy and silent and even mean with her. She was not even allowed to call him Davey. She thought she understood. He had lost his mother. He resented another person taking her place. Margaret backed off. Gave him his space, as the saying went.

But how much space can you give to someone you live with? Someone you love? Was she supposed to let him go out in the cold without his gloves? Was she supposed to send him off to school without pointing out that his fly was open? She gave him what space she could, but matters only got worse.

Their relationship came to be symbolized by a carrot. She left a fresh one, washed and peeled, next to his peanut butter and jelly sandwich for lunch each day. She was careful not to hound him about it. Only once did she mention that carrots were good for him, they supply vitamin A, and, as her own mother had told her time and again, they help one to see in the dark. The daily carrot became her last stand — one small, pitiful, final attempt to bond with her grandson. He never took a bite.

Frustrated, she worked up her nerve for a show-down. She said to him at lunch one day, "We used to have such good times together."

He went on munching his peanut butter and jelly sandwich. The carrot, as usual, lay untouched on the table.

"David?"

Munching. As if she weren't there.

She went away in tears.

Two days later, out of the blue during lunch, an answer arrived: "You were Nana then."

She stiffened. She stood in front of him, looking down on the top of his head, the brown hair she once loved to muss. "*Then?* I still *am* Nana."

"No."

"No?" Something delicate inside her fell from an edge and shattered. She could not keep the tremble from her voice. "What am I now?"

He did not reply. He got up and left the kitchen. A half-eaten sandwich lay on his plate. Sticking up out of the bread, like an orange dagger, was the un-eaten carrot.

Unwilling to add to her son's burden, she kept these things to herself. She bit her lip and counted to ten and reminded herself, he's only a little boy, only a little boy.

So it went for months, and she thought it point-less to even think about going to Midsummer Night's Scream. But then, that one night, she had heard him laughing in his room. "Something funny on TV," he had said, quite pleasantly. And now more recently: all these questions about the Clark Gable picture. Little signs that he was thawing, inching back to his old self. She took courage. She dared to hope it could change.

She chose the same setting as before: the kitchen, lunch. Again he was having peanut butter and jelly. Her nerves were quaking like a girl's. She asked if he would like to go with her to Midsummer Night's Scream.

He said no.

25

Primrose would have swallowed spiders before admitting it, but there was at least one way in which she was like her mother: she enjoyed pretending. Specifically, she enjoyed pretending to be somebody she really wasn't.

She had not done so since Easter morning, when she imitated a dead body in the leaves. Now another chance had come her way. It had begun with a poster she and David had seen at the 7-Eleven checkout counter. It told about the library's Midsummer Night's Scream.

Their first reaction was: "Let's go!" Then Primrose noticed it said "Parent-Child," and David said, "Oh."

Days later David told her his grandmother had asked him to go with her, and he had said no.

"You're not the only one," said Primrose. "It's a problem for me too."

"What do you mean?" said David.

"I mean I'm a kid too. How am I s'pposed get in without *my* mother?"

"So ask her to go with you."

"Yeah, right."

Primrose *was* silent. As she stared at him, a faint smile appeared.

"What?" he said.

"So who says I have to go as the *kid*?"

David stared at her. She could see her meaning sink in. He said nothing. She didn't press it.

Next day she said, "So, what do you think? Me going as a mother?"

He shrugged.

She thought about it. He *wasn't* saying yes, but he *wasn't* saying no either. That put Primrose ahead of his grandmother. She knew deep down he wanted to go. She also knew that out of respect for his mother she shouldn't get too pushy about it.

And then she found herself in a thrift shop, flipping through ladies' clothes, picturing herself. Asking herself: Could I really pull it off?

She could not resist. She bought the clothes. That night she put them on, along with jewelry, makeup, and the final touch: her mother's blonde Madame Dufee wig. She practiced lowering her voice, standing, walking, sitting, waving ("Hi, Mabel!"), laughing, sipping tea. She dressed herself up and tried a test run to 7-Eleven. The girl behind the counter didn't say anything, didn't look at her funny. She thought about trying it on Refrigerator John, but chickened out.

The plan was to keep it out of David's hands. Spring it on him. Let him see her in her mommy outfit, get used to it, see it was no big deal.

So that's what she did the following day. When he came over, she met him at the doorway with the outfit on. She posed. "What do you think?"

He shrugged. "Whatever."

She kept the outfit on while they finished the paint job on the van — white with blue trim on the outside, bright green inside.

A couple of times, stirring paint, she mentioned nonchalantly that as long as she had the outfit, well heck, she might as well use it and go to Midsummer Night's Scream. By herself if need be. What were they going to do, kick her out because she — a mother — showed up without a kid?

"I know you're not going," she said nonchalantly, stirring paint, "but just to let you know, I'll prob'ly have to walk past your house Wednesday night on my way to the library. Prob'ly about eight o'clock." She watched him out of the corner of her eye. He went on painting. He said nothing. He did not seem to have heard.

On Wednesday night, at quarter till eight, he was waiting in front of his house.

The only problem was the navy blue panty hose. They must have been too big, because they kept bagging around her knees and Primrose had to keep hiking them up.

Well, maybe there was one other problem: the high heels. They were murder. She had just bought them today to top off the outfit — ninety-five cents at the thrift shop — and halfway to the library her ankles were sore from all the wobbling. She wished mothers wore skates.

The rest was fine: the powder blue mid-length skirt, white ruffled blouse, navy blazer, pearl necklace, pearl earrings, navy shoulder strap pocketbook, makeup. She had brought the wild blonde wig under control with hair gel. But more than anything else, it was the boy walking beside her, her "son," that completed the outfit.

It surprised Primrose to discover how easy it was to play mother. The *thok-thok* of her high heels upon the sidewalk, the pocketbook brushing her side declared she was a lady, maybe twenty-five, twenty-six. Two blocks from the library, crossing the street, she took David's hand. One block away she said to him with a touch of warning in her voice, as she imagined a mother would do, "Now, you behave tonight. Hear?"

He scowled at her.

Outside the door, she stopped and pulled him around to face her. She cupped his chin in her hand and tilted his face upward. His face was clean, but she rubbed his cheek anyway and clucked her tongue. "I'll bet you didn't brush your teeth either, did you?"

He swatted her hand away. "Knock it off."

She hiked up her panty hose and took him inside. An arrow pointed downstairs to the community room. Hanging over the doorway were fake cobwebs that had to be pushed aside like curtains. Nothing especially scary seemed to be going on. A few little kids were going nuts, otherwise people were standing around munching cookies.

The main thing that struck Primrose was that, except for size, you could hardly tell the mothers from the kids. They were all wearing jeans or shorts, sneakers or sandals. What was the point of being a mother if you didn't look like one? Disgraceful.

As near as she could tell, two fathers were there. They weren't dressed any better, but with them it didn't seem to matter. It hurt to look at them. She turned away.

Somebody approached in an ugly old-hag costume. "Welcome, welcome," said the hag, "As you can see, I am Miss Viola Swamp. And who might you be?"

Primrose cleared her throat and set her voice on low. She put her arm around David. "This is David Limpert. My son."

For an instant Miss Swamp seemed about to cackle hideously, but instead she said, "Good, good. Well, the program will begin shortly. In the meantime" — she waved a bony hand — "help yourself to bug juice and spider cookies. Hee-hee." And off she went.

"This isn't scary," grumbled David. "It sucks."

Primrose grabbed his shoulders. "One more word like that, young man, and you'll get your mouth washed out with soap."

"Yeah?" he sneered. "Who's gonna do it?"

She shook him and whispered hard into his face.

"Don't you *ever* talk to your mother like that."

His eyes locked on hers. To break the tension she gave his nose a motherly tweak and whispered, "Don't have a cow. *We're just pretending.*" When he walked off, she let him go.

She caught a mother looking at her. She shrugged and rolled her eyes and gave a weary smile that said, *These kids, what are we going to do with them?*

She found him at the refreshment table. He had one cookie in his mouth and one in each hand. "Put them down."

"No," he said, spewing crumbs.

She smacked a hand, the cookie fell. "Pick it up."

"No."

No respect, these kids today. Well, they weren't going to walk all over her.

"I said pick it up."

"No."

She smacked the other hand, and the second cookie fell.

137

"Pick."

"No."

She wanted to scream. She wanted to pour the bowl of bug juice over his head. She wanted to ram the cookies down his throat. Everything that came to mind, a mother wasn't allowed to do. So she pinched him.

He howled: "Owwwww!"

He pushed her.

She pushed him.

He screamed, "Don't touch me!"

"I'll touch you all I want!" To prove it, she grabbed him.

"You're not my mother!"

"Yes I am!"

He kicked her in her sore ankle, freeing himself. "No you're not!" he yelled and yanked the wig from her head. He flung it into the gallery of eyes and dashed out through the cobweb curtains.

Minutes later, walking home, Primrose noticed that her steps were getting shorter and shorter. The crotch of her panty hose, she discovered, had come down to her knees. While voices catcalled from passing cars, she tore off her high heels and stockings and left them on someone's front steps.

She walked. She did not know where. She just walked. Only dimly was she aware of the darkening sunset, the streetlights buzzing on, the sidewalks cooling under her bare feet.

Once, at a deserted corner well after dark, she stopped and waved at an imaginary car going by. Not liking the imaginary driver's imaginary response, she yelled, "Oh yeah? You too!" and spit after it.

She never did aim herself home, but eventually she smelled fresh paint and found that she was there. Even before she pulled the van door open she heard snoring. Refrigerator John had rigged up a battery powered lamp for her. She turned it on. Her mother was in her bedroll with Willy the bear, fast asleep.

Primrose cracked.

"Out of my room! This is my room! My place! Out! Out!"

In a flapping flurry of nightgown, her mother fled.

It was not until later, as she was lying down, that Primrose noticed Willy was still there, his white button eyes gawking as if to say, *I don't believe you did that.* She grabbed him by a leg and punched him. She flung him into the street. "Out!"

Who Cares

27

They lived in the same town, but only the sky was vast enough to measure the distance between them.

David rode his bike and spun his yo-yo and watched TV and read *Beetle Bailey*. Read, but did not laugh much.

He rode every day. He no longer rode in circles around town. He rode in straight lines out of town. He rode over the bridge and under the railroad trestle and past the salad-dressing factory and the river and the farm. It was a zoo kind of farm. You were allowed to walk around the pens and stalls and see the animals. Every day at the sheep pen David came upon the same sheep. Every day he felt like punching it in the face.

Thursday nights Primrose went "shopping." On Saturday she peddled her goods at the flea market. The rest of the time she worked on her room.

In his dreams David saw two halves of a worm groping about for each other. One of the halves was bleating, "Davey, where are you?"

As she had long intended, Primrose fixed flower boxes to the side and back windows of her room. In the boxes she planted purple and yellow pansies. She loved the feel of their velvety petals between her fingers.

On one weekend David and his father played miniature golf. Afterward they had Dairy Queen milkshakes. Another weekend they went to a fair. There were warm donuts from a machine. David ate three. They watched goats and cows compete for blue

144

ribbons. The straw on the ground smelled like Madame Dufee's carpet-covered reading room.

August waved shimmering images above the roads he pedaled on. August thundered like falling chairs in a distant room.

Primrose surrounded the van with a one-foot-high white picket fence. The ground in the driveway was hard, so she used a spoon to dig holes for the fence posts.

David became more careful than ever about obeying rules. It was easier to do now that Primrose wasn't around. Sometimes he even made up his own rules — the more to obey, the better. He crossed streets only at corners. He looked both ways. He carried candy wrappers in his pocket for hours until he found a trash can. He never took a shortcut across someone's lawn. He never went in an OUT, out an IN, up a DOWN or down an UP. He never spat on a car. He never stepped on an ant, wiped his hands on his pants, picked his nose, blew bubbles in a drink, said a bad word, flicked earwax, sucked on a shoelace, played in mud, burped on purpose.

Sometimes in the night, when fireflies outside his bedroom window blinked and jiggled like stars on strings, when sleep curled furrily about him, sometimes then he thought he could feel his mother getting closer.

With the help of Refrigerator John, Primrose put a cement birdbath in her picket-fenced front yard. She filled it with water. She backed off a good twenty feet. She looked long at the van that had become her room that had become her home. She borrowed Refrigerator John's camera. She took a picture.

One Saturday morning David's yo-yo string broke. He fitted Spitfire with a new one. The old string he cut into several lengths, which he absently played with as he watched a Bugs Bunny cartoon. When the cartoon was over he looked down at his lap. The strings were braided.

28

The man on the TV screen had shiny black hair piled high and a blue glittery necktie. He sat on a porch, but even David could tell it was a fake porch on a stage somewhere. People were lined up. One person at a time walked up the steps and across the porch and stood before the high-haired, glittery man.

Every one of the people asked the man about somebody who had died, usually somebody in their family — a parent, a child, a grandparent, a wife, a husband. Someone even asked about a parrot. Each one had to tell the glittery man the name of their dead person — or parrot, whose name was Booger. The glittery man asked a few more questions, and then the person forked over something that had belonged to the dead one. Usually it was an item of clothing — a hat, a shoe. The glittery man held the item against his forehead and closed his eyes and swayed and hummed, and when he came out of his trance he told the person that he had been in contact with the "dearly beloved" and that the dearly beloved, even the parrot, had spoken to him. Usually he just heard a voice from beyond the grave — "the Other Side," he called it — but one time he actually saw the dead person. It was someone's wife. The glittery man told the husband what she looked like on the Other Side, and the husband was excited and saying "Yes! Yes! That's her!" and he was crying and laughing at the same time and he practically knocked over the glittery man trying to thank him and hug him, and two bodyguards had to help him off the porch.

29

David chose a Thursday night because he knew Primrose would be out shopping. Even so, he didn't want to risk parking his bike outside and having it seen, so he walked.

As he passed Refrigerator John's abode he was drawn like a moth to the warm windows of light, but he forced himself to keep going. He wished he had brought a flashlight. He wished he ate carrots.

Here the chorus of crickets was loud and never-ending. Every few steps he looked back at Refrigerator John's, its golden windows receding like the portholes of a departing ship. He kept his hands in his pockets. He squeezed the memento.

The house gave no light; darkness seemed to have puddled here. He wanted to turn back, but he had come too far. He found the front door — or rather, the front space. The door was wide open. He reached over the threshold, waved his hand around. Nothing but the smell of sour flowers.

He felt queasy. He whispered, "Hello?"

No answer.

"Anybody home?"

Nothing.

Louder: "Madame Dufee?"

The darkness parted. Someone was coming, a face floating ghostly in candlelight. The face stopped before him. Was it her? He couldn't tell. The wild hair caught in the light was dark, not blonde. Frayed old nightshirt. No flaming dragon tongues. Maybe he came to the wrong house, got mixed up in the dark.

He took a step back.

At last she spoke: "Are you looking for my girl?"

"No," he said. "I'm looking for Madame Dufee."

He looked down at her bare feet. No toe rings. "Are you Madame Dufee?"

She reached into the darkness with the candle. "Is she out there?"

"Who?"

"My girl."

"You mean Primrose?"

She smiled. "Primrose Periwinkle Dufee." *Periwinkle?*

"I want to ask you a question," he said.

"Do you know her? My girl?" She was still looking over his shoulder.

"Yes," he told her.

"She lives out there." She pointed with the candle.

"I know. Madame Dufee —"

"She doesn't sleep with me anymore."

"Madame Dufee!"

He flinched at his own voice, but she continued to gaze at the stars. "Yes?"

"I want to ask you about my mother."

Slowly, for the first time, she turned her face to him. Candlelight glimmered in her eyes and the tips of her wild hair. She smiled. "I know."

"You *do?*"

"Everyone wants to know about their mother. Everyone loves their mother. Do you love your mother?"

"Yes."

"Good boy." She laid her hand on his head. "Your mother will have a long and happy life."

"My mother is dead."

She tilted her head, as if testing the sight of him from a different angle. She closed her eyes. She nodded. "Ah." She stepped aside. "Come in."

He went in and followed instructions to sit opposite her on the floor. In the soft, dim light the room looked more like a tent than ever. She placed the candle between them. They sat like that for a long time. Her eyes were closed. There was a faint smile on her face. Was she making contact with the Other Side? Was his mother there? Here? Somewhere in the shadows beyond the candleglow?

She said, dreamily, "Your mother . . ." She was silent for a while, then said it again: "Your mother . . ."

The candle flame wavered. He felt a spike of excitement. "Do you see her?"

"Your mother . . ."

He clutched his knees. "Carolyn Sue Limpert! She was born in the state of Minnesota! She has brown hair and green eyes!"

She was staring at him. "Green eyes?"

"Yes! Green!"

"My Primrose has green eyes."

He shouted: "My mother! Carolyn Sue Limpert! Is she here?"

Her eyes rolled to the ceiling, beyond the ceiling. "Your mother . . . is everywhere."

Frantically he looked around. "Where?"

"Your mother loves you."

"Where is she? I want to see her."

The shadows, the soft walls were moving. He was standing, turning, reaching . . .

She said, "You were a pretty baby."

He ran from one wall to the next, clutching at the wooly hanging carpets.

"Where is she?"

"My Primrose was a pretty baby."

She was staring at the candle.

He fell to his knees. The candle flame seemed to fatten and grow. It seemed to invite him into the bright heart of itself. She was in here . . . she was close . . .

He pulled the memento from his pocket. It was a little purple plastic turtle. His mother loved turtles. He had bought it for her birthday with his own money. She had made it into a pin. She wore it every day. She was about to be buried with it, but he had reached into the casket and pulled it from her dress, so they wouldn't bury all of her. No one had tried to stop him.

He held out the purple turtle. "This is from my mother." He set it on the carpet.

She ran her fingertip over it. She picked it up. She cradled it in both her hands. She closed her eyes, smiled, sang softly: "Rock-a-bye baby on the treetop . . ."

Dumbfounded, watching her swaying and singing, he knew it was all wrong, he should never have come here. He snatched the turtle from her. "Crackpot!" he shouted. The force of the word blew the candle-point in her direction. "You're a crackpot!"

He ran from the house.

30

He wandered aimlessly, feeling nothing, feeling every-thing. The night was brighter now. The moon was high and round, like a new softball. Cricket sounds puttered like the motors of tiny toys. Faintly sweet and rotten smells came to him from the trash bags and cans lining the curbs. His mother — snippets of memory — fell through the night like summer snow, fell in moonlit whispers: *"Davey . . . Davey . . ."*

In time he wanted only to sleep. He dragged him-self onto a porch. There was a grassy mat in front of the door. It said WELCOME. He lay down on it, curled himself up . . . .

A loud *slap*, and something hit him in the face. He opened his eyes to see a folded newspaper leaning against his nose. A car was accelerating up the street.

The morning paper . . .

The *morning* paper!

He heard his mother's last words to him: *"We'll see the sun rise tomorrow."*

He jumped to his feet, ran to the sidewalk. Across the street, beyond the rooftops of Perkiomen, the sky was pale gray with an unmistakable tinge of pink.

"No!" he shouted. "Not yet!"

He started running before he realized he didn't know which way to go. His house was on Brewster. Where was Brewster? Where was he?

Headlights coming toward him. He stood in the street, waved. The car stopped, the window went down.

"Can you tell me where Brewster Street is?"

The man pointed. "Over there. You okay?"

But David was already running . . . running . . . racing the rising sun, racing down the middle of streets, flying over lawns and flower beds, jamming his eyes to the ground, beseeching the unstoppable sun: "not yet . . . not yet . . ." With every step the night was draining away. He dared look up to get his bearings. Nothing familiar. No Brewster Street. He ran on, flowers colorful smears beneath his flying feet . . . "not yet . . . not yet . . ." Another look up — still no Brewster — but *there* . . . a herd of appliances. Refrigerator John's! He raced to the door, pounded. "Refrigerator! Refrigerator!"

The door opened. Refrigerator stood in boxer shorts and a T-shirt. David burst past him into the living room, dove into the sofa and buried his face in a pillow.

It took some doing, but John finally dragged two pieces of information out of the groggy boy on the sofa: One, he had been out all night, and two, he wanted to sleep. Well, maybe John didn't know much about kids and grandmothers, but he knew about worry, and this kid was going home to do his sleeping in his own bed — now.

The boy went ballistic when John pulled him from the sofa. "No! No!"

He lugged the boy across the room. "Your grand-mother'll be worried sick."

"She doesn't know."

"I don't care. At six in the morning you belong in your own bed."

The boy dug in his heels, clamped his hands over his eyes. "The sun!"

"What about it?"

"Is it up?"

"Sure. It's light out."

The boy clutched his arm. He was frantic. "Go see for sure! Please!"

Was the boy going daffy? John was inclined to just sling him over his shoulder and haul him out of there, but in the end he decided it was less trouble to just do it. He went outside, took a gander, came back in. "Yep. Sun's up. Let's go."

The boy still balked. "All the way? Sunrise is over?"

What was this boy afraid of? "It's over. Next one's not till tomorrow."

He felt the boy relax in his arms. From then on he was no trouble. He climbed into John's truck and went right back to sleep. John knew the address. When they got there, not wanting to wake the boy again, John carried him to the front door and rang the bell.

He had to ring it four or five times before the door finally opened. In the doorway stood a woman hardly taller than himself, clutching a pale blue bathrobe at her throat. His first thought was that she looked much younger than the old crone that David's descriptions had led him to expect. Her hand shot to her mouth and she gasped in wide-eyed shock: "David! Oh my God!"

He tried to smile reassuringly. "It's okay, Mrs. Limpert. He's only sleeping. He's fine."

Her eyes darted from his face to the boy's to the street beyond. She was baffled.

"What —?"

Right there John decided to lie, to spare her what he could. "He just showed up at my house this morning. I guess the birds woke him up and he decided to visit me." He looked at the boy's face, so peacefully sleeping. He wagged his head. "Kids, huh?"

The smile she gave the sleeping boy was loaded with a history he could not read. But he could read the love in her brimming eyes.

"How about if I carry him to his bed?" he suggested.

Her head snapped up. She seemed to see him for the first time. "Yes — I'm sorry. Come in. Come in."

She led him down a hallway to a room in the back of the house. As he deposited the boy in his bed, she laughed and said, "Here you are putting my grandson to bed and I don't even know your name."

"John Daywalt." He held out his hand. She shook

it like a man. "I do appliances. Fix. Sell. Trade. Over on Tulip."

She squinted at him. "Refrigerator John?"

"That's me. And you must be the grandma."

"Margaret Limpert."

They shook hands again.

"Let me get his shoes off," she said, "and we'll go put some coffee on. Can't have morning without it."

"You got that."

And so they talked over coffee in the kitchen. They started off discussing his business and the town and so forth, but pretty soon they zeroed in on the only thing they really wanted to talk about: the boy, David.

"Did you know his mother died?" she said.

He said yes, he knew.

"He was very attached to her."

"I know."

"He still misses her every day."

"I know."

The conversation went on like that until it occurred to him that he better stop saying "I know." He was feeling uncomfortable, guilty even, because he knew so much about her grandson. In some cases more than she did. He wondered if she was aware of how the boy talked about her. If she was aware, she wasn't letting on. She had nothing but nice things to say about her grandson. John admired her for that. He liked her. She had a pleasant, somewhat plumpy face and a full friendly smile. Yes, there was gray in her hair and a crinkle about her eyes, so that a nine-year-old might call her "old," but she was hardly ready for the glue factory. And she was obviously devoted to her grandson. John knew from the boy's talks with Primrose how he treated his grandmother. He knew how it must hurt her. But she did not let it show until they had been talking nonstop for well over an hour. Then she paused and sipped her coffee and looked away. Her smile wilted, and when it came back it was no longer real. "Well, I shudder to think what he must say about his grandmother!" She said it with a laugh and a forced not-that-I-care airiness.

But he wasn't buying it. His heart went out to her. He knew what she was hoping for. She wanted him to refute her fears. She wanted to believe that the boy was unkind only when he was with her, that when he was with other people he spoke of her with affection.

He gave her exactly what she craved. "Hey" — he pumped up two thumbs — "he loves his grandma."

She winced, blinked, brought back the fake smile. She knew he was lying. She reached for his empty cup. "More?" From then on he did most of the talking. He was careful not to say anything that would give away the boy's late-night escapes from his bedroom. He talked about Primrose, about the two of them practically living at his house. As soon as he said "practically living," he regretted it.

It was midmorning when he got up to leave. At the door her smile was real once more, but not quite so big. "Well," she said, "I'm glad he has you two." He shook her hand and walked away and heard the door close softly behind him.

32

Several days later, David woke up to find a note on his bed. It said:

Meet me at my place. Now!

A minute later he was on his bike, wondering, *Is this another trick?* But still pedaling.

She was outside, sunning herself on a lawn chair by a birdbath inside a shin-high white picket fence that surrounded the white and blue van-home. Bare feet. Sunglasses. She did not move as she said, "I stopped over for you. I Baloneyed for you. Where were you?"

The last two weeks, the separation, vanished.

He said, "Shopping for school clothes."

"With your grandmother?"

"Yeah."

He didn't like her in sunglasses, lying there so still. "Is this a trick?"

She got up laughing, wagging her head. "You still think everything's a trick, huh? Well, you're right. I'm gonna . . . *kidnap you!*" She lunged for him. He jumped back. She howled.

"'I still don't like you," he told her.

"Good," she said. "I still don't like you either. And I'm still waiting for you to say something."

"About what?"

She rolled her eyes. "About *what?*" She spun around, thrust her arm toward her new home. "Didn't you happen to notice anything a little different?"

David looked. "Mm, yeah."

"Well?"

"Well what?"

"What do you think?"

He shrugged. "It's okay."

She stared at him. She nodded thoughtfully. "'Okay,' he says." She tapped the fence with her toe. "You're okay? You hear that?" She knocked on the birdbath. "You too, you're okay. That's spelled

165

O-K-A-Y. Did you ever get such a monumental compliment before? I sure didn't. I don't think I can *stand* it. I think I'm gonna *faint*." She struck the back of her hand to her forehead, she swooned. "Oh! . . . Oh! . . ."

Ignoring her, David said, "You got egged." He was looking at three egg splatters on what used to be the back window, now painted white.

Primrose ditched her swoon, led him to the window, and placed his hand on one of the splatters, then the other two. David's eyes bulged. "They're fake!"

"Somebody was selling them at the flea market, along with fake dog poop and vomit. I glued them on."

"Why?"

"I figured, maybe if they see them there, they'll say, Hey, look, she's already egged, let's hit somebody else."

"Did it work?"

"Nope." She snickered. "Sometimes they even come in the daytime now." David could only stare. She shrugged. "I don't care. I got what I want. They're just jealous because of my new place. They wish they could have a place of their own too."

She pulled him around to the door, pushed his head in. "What do you think? Just okay?"

David was amazed. Instead of the bright green paint that he himself had helped to lay on, the interior was covered with wallpaper. There were birthday cakes and kettle drums and prancing horses in feathered bonnets.

"Did I hear you say wow?"

"*Wow*," said David, meaning it.

"I got sick of that green after two days. It was like, *eech!* Fridge took me to the wallpaper place. I picked it out myself." She ducked in for a peek. "Bee-yoo-tiful."

David said, "Is that why you told me to come over?"

Primrose came out with her socks and sneakers. She sat on the lawn chair. "Nope."

David stood over her. "So why?"

Primrose brushed dust from the bottom of her foot and pulled on a sock. "We're going somewhere."

33

Telling him, not even asking.

And what does he do? He follows her like some dumb little puppy dog, till here they are walking along some dumb railroad track, probably get themselves killed, and he *still* doesn't know where they're going.

So for the tenth time he asked her where they were going. This time she answered: "To the city."

"The big city? Philadelphia?"

"Yerp."

David was excited. He had never been to Philadelphia. The only big city he had ever been to was St. Paul, Minnesota. Once. And he heard Philadelphia was bigger than St. Paul.

He was also a little scared. He had never heard of two kids going to a big city by themselves. She was wearing a backpack. He wondered how long they would be gone. He looked back. There was no sign of Perkiomen, only two steel rails going around a bend.

"Why are we going this way?" he said.

" 'Cause I'm not old enough to drive."

"You know what I mean. The tracks."

"It's the only way I know." They were walking on the railroad ties, Primrose stepping on every other one. David had tried it, but the steps were too long for his legs. "I did this before," she said.

"You did?"

"Yeah. Well, not all the way to the city." She stepped up on the rail, her arms out like a tightrope walker. "There's a place up ahead where you can see the skyscrapers."

Skyscrapers. He remembered them from St. Paul. "Is that why we're going? To see the skyscrapers?"

She teetered off the rail. "Nopey dopey."

"So why then?"

She climbed back on. "Tell ya later, gator."

David was getting mad. He hated when she acted goofy like this. "I want to know now."

"Guess you'll just have to trust me," she breezed.

"I *don't* trust you," he growled. "I don't even *like* you." To show her, he pushed her from the rail.

169

She stumbled along the ties, laughing her laugh. When she turned back to him she seemed about to say something, when suddenly her eyes shifted. She was looking past his shoulder. Her eyes were bulging, her mouth a silent scream, and that was all David needed to know to figure out what was coming behind him. And when she cried, "Jump!" and leaped from the tracks, that's what he did too — he jumped.

He landed on his side, he kept rolling, getting as far away as possible, stones digging into his skin. When he came to a stop and dared to look, what he saw was not a thousand-ton train roaring by, but a ropey-haired girl on her hands and knees, heaving so violently that he would have thought she was throwing up if he didn't know she was laughing.

After a while she tried getting upright, staggered tear-blind into the tracks, and fell back to her hands and knees. In time she tested her feet again and found that she could stand. She wiped bucketfuls of tears from her eyes.

"You shoulda seen —," she started to say to David, but he wasn't there. Or there. Or there. Not down the tracks. She turned and looked back the way they came, and there he was, in the distance (How long had she been laughing?), walking the ties between the rails, walking slump-shouldered down the middle of the tracks around the bend. . . .

Around the bend . . . .

"David!" she screamed. She shucked her backpack and took off. In her mind's eye she could see a huge diesel lumbering around the bend, and something told her the dumb clunk had no intention of jumping this time. *"Daviiiid!"*

It took forever to catch up. When she did, she yanked him from the tracks and shook him like a rag doll. "You stupid jerk! What do you think you're doing?"

He screamed back in her face, jaw jutting, hateful: "What do *you* care?".

They glared at each other. She thought he might cry. She thought she might cry. And then she heard the rumble. Felt it first, actually, in the soles of her feet, on her shoulders, then heard it, low and faint as her own heartbeat; then louder, sooner than she would have guessed.

She grabbed him and pulled him farther away, up against a wall of gray rock, David trying to wrench free. She held on tight as the blue face of the engine poked around the trees and the ground trembled and thunder drowned out everything but fear. Ten steps away the train went by, blotting out the world, fanning her face. The first brown leaves of August leaped from the cinder bed and settled at their feet.

The engine grumbled on toward Philadelphia, and soon the only sound was that of boxcars and coal hoppers: the *k-chk k-chk* of their barbelled, pennymashing wheels. When the last car went by, she spat after it in disgust. "Look at that. Not even a caboose."

David squirmed free. They resumed walking, but he kept way ahead of her. She didn't mind, so long as he stayed off the tracks. When he came to her backpack, he gave it a kick.

"You're kicking your own food," she called.

They walked like that for a while, the separation a full block if they had been on a street. They came to another bend in the tracks, a sharp one this time, sharp enough so that suddenly David was out of sight. Primrose clutched her backpack straps and ran — and practically plowed into him. He was standing stone still, staring ahead.

34

At first he thought it was some kind of mountain range, hazy blue with distance. Or giant churches, with their pointy tops.

"There ya go," came Primrose's voice behind him. "The big city. Skyscrapers."

Two of them were way taller than everything else. They speared skyward so high it seemed they would snag the passing clouds.

"We're almost there." She tugged at him. "Come on." He went with her.

She handed him a hoagie, unwrapped one for herself. "Got them at 7-Eleven."

David hadn't realized how hungry he was till he smelled the hoagie. "Aren't we going to stop?"

Primrose bit into hers. "Gotta keep moving. Let

me know when you're thirsty. Look." She held up a bottle of Mango Madness. "One for each of us. A cupcake too."

David had walked while eating before — an ice-cream cone, a candy bar — but never a meal. "Is this lunch?" he said.

"Did you have lunch?"

"No."

"Then it's lunch." She grinned. "At least there's no carrot."

They walked on, eating, staying off the tracks, listening. When Primrose finished her hoagie, she tossed the wrapper. David retrieved it, growled "litterbug," and stuffed it into the backpack. "I don't see the skyscrapers anymore," he said.

"Don't worry," said Primrose, "they're there."

The river, in the distance before, was nearby now, separated from the tracks by only a thin row of trees and viny tangle. They threw stones into it for a while, then they went down to it. Rocks and tree limbs jutted from the water.

"How much farther?" said David.

"Not far," said Primrose.

"You said we were almost there."

174

"I lied."

"How far do we have to go?"

"I don't know. Miles."

"How many?"

"How do I know?"

"Guess."

"Fourteen thousand seven hundred and fifty-two."

They walked on.

"Primrose?"

"What?"

"What would you rather get hit with, an egg or a stone?"

"What kind of question is that?"

"I don't don't, just a question."

"It's stupid."

"I'd rather get hit with an egg. It splats all over you and makes an icky mess, but it doesn't hurt like a stone."

"That's what you think."

Farther on, David looked at the shrubs lining both sides of the tracks.

"Primrose?"

"Now what?"

"What if we get jumped?"

"Attack 'em with your yo-yo."

The day had been such an adventure, David had not until now thought of his yo-yo. He drew Spitfire from its holster.

"Want me to teach you stuff?"

"Not really."

David worked on his stunts, made even harder because he was walking at the same time. Then he had a great idea: walk the dog on the track! He stepped on the ties, snapped Spitfire down to the end of the line and laid it gently on the smooth steel rail, itself barely wider than the many-colored spool. Spitfire jumped off. It jumped a second time. He kept trying until finally he had it going, a spinning blur, runaway wheel of a rainbow train riding the silver rail. "Primrose, look!"

Primrose looked. He half-expected her to make fun of him or say he was being stupid, but she didn't. She just looked and nodded and said, "Cool." Then she said, "Can I try?"

David wound up the yo-yo and slipped it onto her finger. He laughed at her fumbling efforts. She couldn't even make Spitfire sit down, much less walk. He took Spitfire back and showed her how a real pro did it. Then he spotted a weed with a fuzzy white top. "Watch this."

He returned Spitfire to its holster. He stood gunfighter style, facing the weed, scowling, feet apart, knees slightly bent, hands at his sides holster-high, fingers spread, fingertips tingling. "Say when."

"When."

In less than three seconds, maybe two — "Bam!" — Spitfire was zinging on a laser line. The fuzzy weed top exploded.

"Not bad," said Primrose, "for an infant."

She picked out a fuzz-topped weed for herself. She stood before it gunfighter style, scowling, fingertips twitching. "Say when."

"When."

She reared back and spit — "Ptool!" Fuzz flew.

David clapped. "Good shot! Let's mow 'em all down!"

They went from weed to weed: "Bam!" — "Ptool!" — "Bam!" — "Ptool!" — laughing, obliterating cotton tops till Primrose ran out of juice. It took a minute for her mouth to relube so she could talk right. "I coulda gone longer if I had a jawbreaker."

"Why?" said David.

"They make good spit."

They walked on.

Primrose said, "Did you miss me the last couple weeks?"

"No."

"Me neither."

Later she said, "What did you do?"

David shrugged. "Stuff."

Primrose chuckled. "I had fun."

David chuckled. "Me too."

Primrose wagged her head. "I had so much fun — whew! — I could hardly stand it."

"Me too," said David. "I had so much fun I almost got sick."

"Yeah?" said Primrose. "Well I really *did* get sick one day. I went to the doctor, and he examined me and said" — she made her voice low — "'You are all worn out, young lady. Looks to me like you OD'd on fun.' He said I had to slow down or I'd give myself a heart attack."

"Me too," said David.

They rounded a curve, and again the two sky-scrapers appeared before them, only this time they were different. The entire right sides, all the way up to the arrow-tip tops, were aglow. It was one of the most beautiful things David had ever seen. "Look," he said, pointing, "they're golden."

"Yeah," she said. "And bad news too."

"Huh?"

"That's not gold. It's the sun shining off the windows."

David looked at her. "So?"

"So the sun's going down. So it's getting late."

Suddenly David felt cool. "You mean, like, dark?"

She snickered. "Yeah. Like dark."

He stared at her. "Can't we make it before dark?"

She didn't answer.

35

"I want to go home."

"That's the hundredth time. Don't say it again."

"I want to go home."

Primrose stopped. She grabbed him by the shoulders and turned him around. "You want to go home? Fine. Go." She pushed him.

David stumbled forward a few steps and stopped. He balled his fists and wailed down the empty tracks, which were totally in shadow now: "I hate you!" He picked up a stone. He turned.

She picked up a stone. Hers was bigger.

"You wouldn't throw that at me," he said.

She grinned. "No?"

"I'm just a little kid. You said."

"A little kid with a stone in his hand."

"Who said I was gonna throw it?"

"Good," she said. "So drop it."

He had gone too far to drop it.

He swung his arm back. "I'm just gonna lob it, that's all."

She swung her arm back, she grinned. "Lob away."

"Listen, *wait* —," he said. He was boxed in. He knew it. And he could think of only one way out. "I know something about you, and it's something you don't want to know, and if you throw that at me I'm gonna tell you anyway and you're gonna feel really bad." He studied her. Did she believe him? Did he believe himself? "Okay?" She said nothing. "Look — I'm just gonna lob it. Here goes —" He lobbed the stone softly in a high arc; it fell harmlessly in front of her.

She reared back and fired her stone. It bit the ground at his feet and sent a spray of gravel against his ankle.

"You asked for it!" he yelled. But he never found out if he really would have told her, because she said, grinning smugly, "The guy in the picture isn't my father."

David stood dumbstruck. "How did you know?"

"Found out a couple years ago. I guess my mother made up all that stuff about my father. Anyway, I figured, who cares? Whoever he was, he's sure as heck not here. Is he?" She made a mock show of looking around. "So ever since then I've just been" — she waved blithely and walked off — "pretending."

David ran to catch up. "But don't you feel bad?"

"Not really," she said. "Pretending works."

They walked on.

The golden skyscrapers were out of sight again. David kept looking at the sky, which was still a friendly blue. With trees on one side and high gray stone bluffs on the other, it seemed he was walking in a box with the lid off.

"I'm hungry," he said.

Primrose checked the backpack. She pulled out the remaining items. "One chocolate cupcake. One inch of Madness, left in *my* bottle. But because I am such a fantastically nice person, I'm willing to share. One opened pack of chocolate malt balls, with" — she counted — "nine left."

"I didn't know you had malt balls."

"I didn't either. I think they've been in here since last Christmas." She held one out to him. "Want?"

David stared at it, took it, smelled it, stared again, opened his mouth. Primrose barked: "Wait!" She snatched the malt ball from him.

182

"Hey!"

"Sorry," she said. "I just remembered. This stuff will make you thirsty. We each have a half inch of Madness left. We can't be getting thirsty."

Streams of saliva flooded David's mouth. He had never craved anything in his life as much as he craved that malt ball. He reached for it. She pulled it away. She stuffed the malt balls and everything else in the backpack and zipped it shut.

"I'm hungry," he whined. He reached for the pack.

She smacked his hand. "We'll eat later. We have to save it."

"I'm hungry *now*."

"You won't be if you stop saying it. Think about something else."

David tried, but now that his stomach had gotten his attention, it wouldn't let go. Suddenly he had an idea. *Buy some food!*

She pulled her pockets inside out. "Broke."

"Broke? How can you be broke? You always have money. You're rich."

"I spent the last dollar on wallpaper and food for today. And anyway, you see a 7-Eleven around here?"

David let out a yawp of frustration. He kicked stones. "I'm hungry. I'm thirsty. I want to go home."

He scowled at her. "It's all your fault." He kept scowling.

She smiled.

"How far do we have to go yet?"

"Don't know."

"How are we getting back home?"

"Beats me."

"Are we gonna be out all night?"

"Yerp."

He jumped in front of her, planted his feet, screeched up at her: "You don't even *care*. *Do you?*"

She smiled — "Nerp" — and hip-swung around him.

With the balled bottom of his fist he thumped her on the arm, then jumped back. She strolled on, not even glancing at him. He dared again: thump, jump back. She was smiling and humming. "I hate you! I hate you!" he shrieked and hit her once more, this time not holding back because she was a girl, this time knuckles first.

She snickered. "That's the hardest you can hit?" Snooty and grinny above him, she strolled on, whistling.

Only Children

36

They were walking on the land side of the tracks, under the stone bluffs. Above, they could see the occasional back end of a shingled building, broken windows, a fragment of fence. They walked in a world of cindery gray.

"When are you going to tell me where we're going?" said David.

"We're going to Philadelphia."

"I know. I mean why."

"Can't say yet."

David groaned under the pain of unanswered questions.

"I'm afraid," she said.

David couldn't believe it. Primrose? Afraid?

"What of?"

She made a scrunchy, lemon-sucking kind of face. "I don't know. Afraid to say it, I guess. Out loud. It sounds so goofy."

"Just tell me. I won't think it's goofy."

"Maybe later."

David groaned. He was still groaning and complaining when suddenly Primrose yelled, "Look out!" and snatched him and lunged for the tracks as a pair of fat black plastic trash bags bumped down the bluff to the ground. On impact, they split open, spilling contents.

Primrose screamed to the bluff top: "Jerks!" She headed for the bags. She found a stick and began poking through the spillage. "Don't touch anything," she warned. "Who knows what germs those jerks have." She yelled again, straight up: "Coulda killed us!"

"Prim, look," said David. He pointed to a comic book, its back cover showing. "Can I pick it up?"

She worked the stick between the pages and lifted it. She inspected it. "Go ahead."

David took the comic. "Phooey. It's *Veronica*."

"*Veronica?* I'll take it." She put it in her backpack. She found nothing else worth taking. She gave a parting yell: "Cheapskates!"

When she turned she found David sitting on a railroad tie. She snapped her fingers. "Let's go, Moe."

"I'm not going anywhere till I eat," he said.

She took a deep breath. She looked up. The sky's blue was now darker than that of the painted trim on her new house. Across the river, lights were on. "All right," she said. "Might as well stop for the night anyway. Let's look for a good place."

They crossed the tracks to the river side. It wasn't long before David realized he didn't know what he was looking for. "What's a good place?" he asked.

"A clear space," she said, "not too big, just for the two of us, bushes all around."

It took another ten minutes of walking and looking before Primrose decided on a place, midway between tracks and water.

"These bushes aren't all around us," David said. Primrose set down her backpack. "They're between us and the tracks. That's what counts."

"Why does that count?"

"So people can't see us from the tracks."

David stared at her. "What people?"

"Who knows? All kinds of weird people walk the tracks at night."

David let out a fearful cry.

"Stop worrying," said Primrose. "That's what the bushes are for, so nobody sees us."

David cringed. "I'm scared."

Primrose inspected the ground for bugs and sat down. "Just pretend we're fugitives. We escaped from jail and they're out there looking for us, but they can't find us because we're in this great hideout."

"I don't want to pretend," he whined.

Primrose took out the chocolate cupcake, broke it, and held out half. "Here, pretend you're hungry."

David snatched the cupcake and stuffed it into his mouth. He swallowed it nearly whole. Primrose stared, her empty hand still out. David plucked a crumb from it.

"That," said Primrose, "was really stupid. You should make it last."

With her front teeth she clipped a bit of chocolate icing from her half. She sucked on it and closed her eyes and went, "Mmmm." Then she clipped another bite.

"I want more," said David.

"Wait till I'm done eating my cupcake," said Primrose.

It took her ten minutes.

"I want my drink," said David.

"The drink comes last. We each have about two swigs, and that has to last till morning. So we do all our eating first, then we drink."

David held out his hand. "Malt ball."

She gave him one. A crunch of teeth, a swallow — gone.

Primrose chose. "One for me." She smelled it, she kissed its smooth chocolate coating, she rolled it over her cheeks and up and down her nose. She placed it on her tongue and closed her mouth over it. She closed her eyes and went, "Mmm . . . mmm . . ." When it reappeared, displayed between her front teeth, it was slightly smaller and off-white, its chocolate jacket gone. Back into her mouth it went, where it tumbled and crunched until, with a satisfied "Ahh" she said, *That's* how to eat a malt ball."

"How *you* eat," said David. "How many are left?"

She counted. "Seven."

"Give me" — he figured — "four."

"Three. Owner gets the extra. She counted out three. "You sure you want them now?"

He held out his hand. She gave them to him. He shoved all three into his mouth and chewed like a cement truck till they were gone. He held out his hand. "Drink."

Primrose got the bottle. She wagged her head. "Dumb . . . dumb . . ." She studied the remaining inch of Mango Madness. With a malt ball, she made a small chocolate mark at the halfway point.

David reached. "Oh no," she said. "Keep your hands down. *I'll* hold it. *I'll* pour."

David grumbled but complied. She set the bottle to his lips and tilted it. He swallowed, but mostly what he got was air, a trickle in a canyon.

"Hey," he said.

"Sip," she said.

They did it twice more. Primrose checked the bottle. "That's it," she announced. She showed him. The Mango Madness was down to the chocolate mark.

"I hardly tasted it," he whined. "That didn't even add up to a whole swallow. You cheated."

Primrose capped the bottle and returned it to the backpack. "I probably tricked you, right?"

"Yeah, you did."

"Well, you'll just have to pardon *moi* while I eat the rest of my dinner." She sniffed another malt ball. Like a dog at a kitchen table, David sat and stared, his eyes going from her hands to her face, as she took ten forevers to devour three malt balls. Most of the time she had her eyes shut. When she opened them for good with a final "Ahhh!" she rubbed her stomach and sighed. "That was one of the biggest meals I ever had. I am positively *stuffed.*"

She pushed herself grunting to her feet. She swayed, holding her stomach, bloating her cheeks. "Don't know if I can walk." She waddled past him, brushing bushes, groaning, "Oh, I'm stuffed . . . never again . . ."

The next time he heard her voice, it was different: "David."

He rose, he turned, and at once he knew what had happened. They had been so busy fussing at each other that they hadn't noticed. She was a shadow in a world of shadows. He went to her. Here, there, up and down the river, solitary lights nested in the dark. Somewhere a train whistle hooted, or was it something else?

He came closer. He clutched her shirt.

"Night's here," she said.

37

They talked.

They talked because it was night, and because weird people walk the tracks at night, and because there was nothing else to do, and because they could barely see each other, and because maybe the bushes were not enough.

The sound of their voices was a palisade against the dark.

At last Primrose told David why they were going to the city: "To see the waving man."

He was stunned. "The one on TV? That waves at cars?"

"Yeah."

"Why?"

"Don't laugh."

"I won't."

"Two reasons."

"Yeah?"

"Number one, I want to see if it's fake."

"You think it's a trick?"

"Not a trick exactly. Well, maybe. I don't know. That's the problem, I don't know. I want to find out for sure. See it for myself."

"What's number two?"

"Don't laugh."

"I *said.*"

"I'm gonna ask him why he does it."

"Really?"

"Yeah. *If* it's real, I'm gonna ask him."

"What do you think he'll say?"

"How do I know? That's why I'm asking."

David said, "I have a question too."

"Yeah? What?"

"I was thinking about it for a long time."

"Are you going to tell me?"

"Do you have to be in a car for him to wave to you?"

Primrose did not know.

She said, "How long did you know about the picture?"

He said, "I don't know. A pretty long time."

"How did you find out?"

"At the flea market one day. Somebody was selling lots of them. They gave me one for free, but no frame. I showed it to my grandmother. She told me."

"Your grandmother, huh?"

"Yeah."

"Did she laugh? Say I was stupid?"

"I didn't tell her it was about you."

"And you didn't tell me."

"No."

"You didn't think I knew it wasn't really my father."

"No."

"But you didn't tell me."

"No."

"Why not?"

"I don't know."

"When *were* you going to tell me?"

"I don't know."

"But then you got mad at me."

"Yeah."

"And so you were going to tell me."

"I was just kidding."

"It was a just a threat, right?"

"Yeah."

"Would you never have told me?"

"I don't know."

"As long as you lived?"

"I don't know."

"Prob'ly not, huh?"

"Prob'ly."

David could not see her face, but he knew she was crying. He wondered why.

"Primrose?"

"Huh?"

"I know another secret."

"About me?"

"No. Me."

"You gonna tell me, or do I have to beg?"

"I won't ever see the sun rise unless I'm with my mom."

"Because you were going to see it with her, but then she fell and hit her head and died the day before. April twenty-ninth. Carolyn Sue Limpert. Slippery floor. Minnesota."

"You know all that?"

"You only told me a million times. Me and Fridge."

"I wish Refrigerator John was here."

"We're okay."

Their words held hands in the night.

"Primrose?"

"Huh?"

"I have another secret, that you *really* don't know about."

"Yeah?"

"Yeah. You want to hear it?"

"No."

Silence.

She laughed. "Just kidding."

"I'm afraid to tell it."

"It's about your mother."

He gasped. "How did you know?"

"A totally wild guess."

"It's my most secretest secret there is."

"You have till the count of three. One . . . two . . ."

"I believe that if I obey all the rules, my mother will come back."

"Is that why you're always picking up litter?"

"Yeah."

"Why you never go in the Out at the supermarket?"

"Yeah."

"You really believe it, huh?"

"Yeah. Why, you think it's stupid?"

"Believe what you want. It's a free country."

David tore a weed from the cool earth. "What if it is stupid?"

"What're you asking me for? What do I look like, a professor or something? I'm thirteen years old. I'm a kid."

"Or what if I'm just not good enough? What if my mother's waiting someplace, just *waiting* for me to be good enough so she can come back, but she can't because I keep messing up." He punched his leg with each word. "Messing up . . . messing up . . ."

He was crying.

Primrose said, "Hold out your hand."

He felt her hand touch his, turn it palm up. Then he felt something smooth and round. "Malt ball?"

"The extra one. I saved it."

"For me?"

"Eat it."

He ate it.

"Hold out your hand."

He did. Now it held a bottle.

"There's just a sip left. You can't eat a malt ball without drinking something afterward." She snickered. "It's a rule."

He drank. She *was* right, it was just a sip, finished even as his mouth was reaching for more. But it was the most wonderful sip he had ever had.

And then, suddenly, he could see her.

She was looking up, pointing. "Moon's out."

Out it was, a little lopsided, like a deflated volleyball, unmoving among the smoky drift of clouds.

She reached into her backpack and came out with the *Veronica* comic. She wagged it in his face.

"Quick," she said, "read to me."

"It's dark," he said.

"Use the moonlight. You can do it. C'mon, before it goes back in. Wait — " She pulled off her sneakers and socks. She flattened the socks and lay them neatly one atop the other on the ground. She lay herself down then, on her back with her head pillowed on the socks. "Okay, go."

David opened the comic book. "I can't. It's too dark."

"That's what you get for not eating your carrots. Turn around, so the moon's behind you."

David did so. She was right. The moon, like a lamp over his shoulder, gave light enough to see the words.

"Wait!" Primrose pulled David's legs out in front of him, flat to the ground, then swung herself around so that her head rested in his lap. "Okay, now, go, go, go."

David began to read.

Primrose interrupted. "Read the ads too."

David snapped, "O-*kay*. Now shut up."

He read on. He read a story about Veronica's birthday and the plan she came up with to make Archie buy her the present she wanted most. He didn't understand all the words, but that was all right because all he had to do was pronounce them, and he was good at that. He was especially good at sound effects, such as "Krrr-rash!" and "Oof!" His favorite character turned out to be neither Veronica nor Archie, but Ms. Beazly, the wild-haired lunchroom lady. She was so crotchety to everybody, even the principal, she made David laugh.

When he finished the birthday story, he lifted the comic and looked down at Primrose. Her eyes were closed. There was a faint smile on her face, the same face he had brushed leaves from in the park. Her hands were folded over her chest, like his mother's in the funeral parlor. He didn't like that. He lifted one of her hands as gently as possible and moved it. And noticed something else too — ugly bruises on the moonwashed surface of her arm — where he had punched her. He whispered, "Primrose." She did not move.

He read some more. He was partway through the next story, about Veronica's job at an ice-cream shop, when the light went out. A cloud had covered the moon.

"David?"

"Huh?"

"What happened?"

Her voice was groggy, her eyes still closed.

"The moon went in. I thought you were asleep."

"I was. You stopped."

"It's out again. Go back to sleep."

She moved her head from his lap and lay on her side on the ground. The moon was not out again, but that was no matter. David knew now what to do. He raised the comic book. He began: "So, Veronica was supposed to make a banana split, but she couldn't find any bananas, so . . ." Word by word he made up the story, turning the pages noisily as if he were reading. He made sure to have Ms. Beazly visit the ice-cream shop.

When he finished that story he made up another, about Veronica enlisting in the army and meeting Beetle Bailey.

Then he told the story of Mike Mulligan and his steam shovel named Mary Anne. He remembered every word as his mother had read it to him night after night.

He told the story of *Goldilocks and the Three Bears*. And then he retold it as *Beetle Bailey and the Three Bears*. And then as *Mike Mulligan and the Three Bears*. And then as *Ms. Beazly and the Three Stooges*. That one gave him lots of *oofs* and *krrr-rushes*.

He had never known he had so many stories in him. Whenever the moonlight came back — a minute here, a minute there — he used it to look at her. She was as asleep as a person ever was. She was catching up on a lifetime without bedtime stories, and David was determined to give her a thousand nights' worth.

The Little Engine That Could.

Jack and the Beanstalk.

The Little Beanstalk That Could.

A Steam Shovel Named Primrose.

And then, his own eyes drooping, he told his final story. It was called *David and His Mother*. It was about a boy who lost his mother. All because somebody made a dumb mistake and didn't follow a rule. And so the boy decides to follow a thousand rules of his own. Maybe a million. And sooner or later that broken rule will be mended and his mother will come back. Then he meets this girl with ropey hair, a teenager, and she breaks every rule she runs into and moves out of her own house to get away from her mother — and it's just all backwards, this story, because the kid who wants a mother doesn't have one and the one who has one moves out. He wants to scream at the girl, "You don't know how lucky you are!" but instead he goes to see her mother, who is a fortune-teller, and she tricks the boy into thinking she can bring his mother back but she can't because she's a crackpot. But she loves her daughter, David can tell, loves her the way David's mother loved him, and sometimes David feels that same love he used to, except now it's coming from other places, other people, and it's a good thing the love is coming because he's beginning to think there aren't enough rules in the universe to bring his mother back.

By the time he finished the story he was lying down beside her. A distant train whistle flew up the moon-silver river like a long last good-bye. He squirmed backward, fitting himself into the spoon of her body. He reached back for her arm and pulled it over and around himself. He closed his eyes, and then there was nothing but the sound of her breathing in his ear.

38

"David, wake up."

Mom?

"Wake up!"

She was shaking him.

He opened one eye. "Huh?"

"C'mon, I want to show you something. Come *on.*" She pulled him to his feet. "It's neat. You gotta see." She dragged him by the hand, chattering. "I woke up really early. I wasn't even tired. You were out like a light. I figured I'd go do some exploring. Watch your step here."

All was gray, like before. The river was gray, still and flat and gray. He did not want to watch his step. He wanted to sleep. He stepped in water.

"See that," she growled. "You never listen." She stopped and sat him down and pulled off his sneaks and socks and rolled up his pant legs to his knees. "Leave your stuff here. We'll get it on the way back. C'mon."

He staggered on, hand-dragged, almost awake now. "Where are we going?" he whined.

"You'll see. We're almost there. Around this bend."

The river turned left. As they came out of the turn David could once again see the pair of sky-scrapers beyond the trees. But it was the river that caught his attention. It was even wider here and very straight. In fact, in the distance, he could see the river meet the sky, which was blushing at that point. Several bridges spanned the river, framing the rosy horizon. Closer to them something else crossed the water.

Primrose pointed. "There it is."

"What is it?" David said. It was long and narrow and flat, barely higher than the water, the color of concrete. It looked like a sidewalk from one river-bank to the other.

"A dam," she said. "C'mon."

Across the river a lightbulb winked out.

David said, "What time is it?"

She grabbed her wrist. "What do I look like, a clock? Come on." She was running, pulling him along, his bare feet slapping water. The blush in the sky was getting brighter by the second.

They stopped at the edge of the dam. She threw out her arms. "Neat, huh?" She looked pleased and proud enough to have discovered America.

"Usually, see, the water runs over it. But the river's low." She reached down and ran her hand over the pitted surface of the dam. "Dry as a bone." She stepped onto it. "We can walk across!" She pulled David on.

The surface was rough and cool on his bare feet. The sky at the end of the river was no longer blushing, it was glowing from the fire below. He wrenched free. "No!" he yelled. "I can't! You *know* I can't! I *told* you!"

She looked at the horizon, looked at him. She snatched his wrist. "Listen, you little mouse nipple, I'm walking across this river and you're coming with me. If you don't want to look, fine, don't look."

She yanked him forward. There was no escaping her grip. He closed his eyes, squeezed them shut, and remembered walking down the dark hallway behind his mother the night the electricity went out. As on that night, fears he could not name blew chills upon him from a window left open to his soul. But there was no fear in his feet, for they trusted utterly the hand that led him.

In time she stopped.

Were they across?

"Primrose?" he said.

She jerked his hand. "Shh."

He could tell that she had turned. She was facing downriver. They were still on the dam. When her voice finally came, it was hardly a whisper, hardly hers: "Oh wow . . . oh my God . . . oh man . . ."

Her hands cupped his shoulders, gently turned him. At once he felt it on his face: the warmth, the newborn day.

"Okay," she said, her voice sweet as Mango Madness. "You don't have to look. I won't make you."

Her hands fell away. He was alone. Untouched.

A voice deep inside, a David-voice from long ago, cried out to the Other Side: "Mommy!" But he knew the time had come. He opened his eyes and followed the river to the crown of the rising sun. It was crisp and sharp and beautiful and smooth as a painted egg. And changing by the moment. Orange at first, then butterscotch, then yellow, a plump breakfast yellow of egg yolk; and then, as if poked with a fork, it suddenly broke, spilling, flooding the river and the city and the trees and the sky and every dark corner of the world.

He had been tricked again. But this time it was different, this time it was okay. He clung to her, sobbing, his tears damp on her shirt, nearly squeezing the breath out of her.

She folded him in her arms. "I'm not her, you know," she whispered hoarsely. "I'm only me. Primrose."

He nodded against her. "I know."

39

They were still there, sitting cross-legged in the middle of the dam, when the policeman came. He stood on the river bank and called: "David Limpert? Primrose Dufee?"

"Yes!" they called.

"Time to go home!"

The policeman let them sit up front in the patrol car. He gave them a bag of pretzels to eat. He let them drink iced tea from a Thermos bottle under his seat. He showed them the buttons for the overhead flashers and the siren.

Though it was hard to do sitting down, David showed him a Spitfire quick-draw. The policeman nodded. "Very impressive." He said maybe he would trade in his gun for a yo-yo. David laughed.

"How long were you looking for us?" David said.

"Since last night," said the policeman. "Where were you all this time?"

"Walking the tracks. We were going to Philadelphia."

"That's a long way to walk."

David crunched a pretzel. "Yeah, I know. And we made a camp in the bushes and we went to sleep on the ground. And all we had to eat was malt balls and a cupcake and about two sips of Mango Madness. Two *sips*!"

"It's a wonder you survived."

David nodded. "It's a wonder."

Primrose said, "Who called the police?"

"Don't know," said the policeman. "The call came in at Perkiomen, where you live. They sent it out to the other stations."

David's eyes boggled. "An all points bulletin?"

"More or less."

"All *right*!"

The policeman glanced over David's head at Primrose. "I'm sure whoever called will be waiting for you there."

They were still a block away when the crowd of

people came into view. "Your welcoming committee," said the policeman. "Shall we let them know you're coming?" He pointed to the flasher button.

David punched it, but something else was on his mind. He reached deep into his pocket. "Primrose," he said.

She looked down and saw in his hand a little plastic purple turtle. He was holding it between himself and her so no one else could see.

She whispered, "The memento?"

He nodded.

A gentle bump, a swerve: they were in the parking lot.

"You're not allowed to wear it," he said. "But I'll let you hold it for a day."

She cleared her throat. She smiled into his wide eyes. "You keep it." She folded his fingers over it. "I'll always remember I saw it."

He put it away. He looked up at her. "I read you to sleep."

She closed her eyes, she nodded. "You read me to sleep."

Click! Lock buttons sprang up. The doors opened to a burst of applause and cheers. Running toward them were David's grandmother and Refrigerator

212

John and a man Primrose assumed was David's father. All wore faces wild with joy, celebrating faces, crying and laughing faces. Primrose had expected no less. What she had not expected was her mother, out in front of them all, lunging clumsily toward them, her eyes every bit as wild as the others', her zany blonde wig falling over her ear.

40

"Primrose."

"Of course. Primrose."

"Refrigerator John."

"Refrigerator John."

They were sitting at the kitchen table, David and his grandmother. David's birthday was coming up in fourteen days, and there was going to be a party. Between munches on a carrot, David was saying who should be invited. His grandmother was writing down the names.

"Adam Tuggle."

"Adam Tuggle? Who's that?"

"The policeman who found us. He let me work the cop-car lights."

"Adam Tuggle it is." She wrote down the name.

"How about me? Do I get invited?"

It was David's father, coming into the kitchen. He plopped himself down on David's lap. It didn't really hurt, because his father was holding himself up, but David knew his part was to cry out in pain, so that's what he did. "Oww!" His dad gasped in mock shock —

"Oh, sorry" — got up, reversed the arrangement, and now David was sitting on his dad's lap.

Almost-ten David knew he was getting too old to sit on laps, but he didn't care. He was still swooning in amazement: his father was home and it wasn't even the weekend! He had driven straight from Connecticut the minute he heard David was missing. He said they were going to spend more time together now. In fact, they were going to a ball game in the city tonight.

His grandmother was giving them her smile across the kitchen table. For some reason, David didn't find it annoying anymore. "How about Tim?" she said.

David was stumped. "Who's Tim?"

"The boy with the yo-yo. We met him that day on the street, remember?"

"He stunk," said David. "He couldn't even walk the dog. He's a geek."

"He's a nice boy," said his grandmother. "He was *very* impressed with you. I've seen him around the

215

neighborhood. I'm sure he would like to be your friend."

His father tickled him, made him laugh. "Hey, then I'm a geek too. I stink with a yo-yo."

"You don't judge a person on how good they are with a yo-yo," said his grandmother. "He might turn out to be the coolest kid you ever knew, but you're not giving him a chance."

This was a shock, hearing his grandmother say "coolest." She was surprising him a lot lately. And he had to admit they both made good points about the kid named Tim. Plus, he was already out of names to invite. Since moving to Perkiomen from Minnesota, he had made no new friends except for Primrose and Refrigerator. Of course he could have, but he just hadn't felt like it.

He gave a sigh. "Okay. Put him down."

Then he thought of one more. "And Madame Dufee."

His grandmother looked up. "Primrose's mother?"

"Yeah."

She gave him the smile. "That's nice. She'll be happy."

"She's goofy."

"David. Don't be unkind."

"I mean in a funny way," he said. *And she loves her Primrose Periwinkle*, he thought. He said to his dad, "She's a fortune-teller. She can read your hand. Even your foot! She'll tell you —" He caught himself. Let Madame Dufee be the one to tell his dad he'd have a long and happy life.

"Tell me what?" said his dad.

"Never mind," he said, smiling secretly. "You'll see."

After the game that night, seat-belted into the passenger side for the ride home, David felt the drowsies overtaking him. Time too. In two weeks he would leave nine behind for good. Something in him did not want to move on, wanted to go back to eight, stay eight forever with his mother. But time was like that freight train, carrying him onward to ten and eleven, carrying him down the tracks and around the bend whether he liked it or not.

He felt the tiny turtle in his pocket. He still heard his mother's voice — "Davey" — rise like whisper-dust from unseen corners in the house, but it was no longer the only voice he heard. His ears were also filled with the voices of others — his father and Primrose and Refrigerator John and his grandmother. Of course, all of their words for a thousand years could not fill the hole left by his mother, but they could raise a loving fence around it so he didn't keep falling in.

4

The question came to him three nights later as he was lying down to sleep. Earlier in the summer he would have simply put on his clothes and snuck out the back window. Now, he waited till morning.

As he pulled his bike up to her place, he saw a bulge of black-on-white polka dots — the beanbag chair — pop from the side door and onto the ground. Primrose, puffing, stepped out after it. "You're just in time," she said. "You can help me lug this monstrosity into the house."

David looked inside the van. He was stunned. "It's empty!"

She flicked sweat from her eye. "I'm moving back." She bent over the chair. "Get the other side."

David went to the other side. "There's something I forgot to ask you, and I just remembered."

She stood, hands on hips. "Make it fast. I can't move unless I'm in the mood, and this mood's got about ten seconds to go."

David spoke quickly. "We never got to Philadelphia to ask the waving man why he waves. Are we still going?"

"No need to."

"No?"

"Nope. I figured it out myself. I know why he waves to people."

"You do? Why?"

She bent over. "You're stalling." She grabbed the bottom of the chair. "Lift and I'll tell you. On three."

David snapped off a chunk of the carrot he was carrying, stuck the rest in his pocket, and grabbed hold of the chair.

"One, two, *three.*" The chair rose unsteadily from the ground. "Because," she grunted, "they wave back."

The great, lumpy black-and-white polka-dotted beanbag wobbled toward the house.